AWU'S STORY

Histoire d'Awu

AWU'S
STORY

A NOVEL

JUSTINE MINTSA

Translated and with an
introduction by Cheryl Toman
Foreword by Thérèse Kuoh-Moukoury

UNIVERSITY OF NEBRASKA PRESS   LINCOLN AND LONDON

Awu's Story was first published in
French as *Histoire d'Awu,* © Éditions
Gallimard, Paris, 2000
Translation © 2018 by the Board of
Regents of the University of Nebraska

Publication of this volume was assisted by a
grant from Case Western Reserve University.

Library of Congress
Cataloging-in-Publication Data
Names: Mintsa, Justine Elo, author. | Toman,
Cheryl, translator, writer of introduction. |
Kuoh-Moukoury, Thérèse, writer of foreword.
Title: Awu's story: a novel / Justine Mintsa;
translated and with an introduction by Cheryl
Toman; foreword by Thérèse Kuoh-Moukoury.
Other titles: Histoire d'Awu. English
Description: Lincoln: University
of Nebraska Press, [2018]
Identifiers: LCCN 2017044660
ISBN 9781496206930 (pbk.: alk. paper)
ISBN 9781496208064 (epub)
ISBN 9781496208071 (mobi)
ISBN 9781496208088 (pdf)
Subjects: LCSH: Gabonese fiction
(French)—Translations into English.
Classification: LCC PQ3989.3.M535 H5713
2018 | DDC 843/.92—dc23 LC record
available at https://lccn.loc.gov/2017044660

Set in Scala by E. Cuddy.
Designed by N. Putens.

CONTENTS

FOREWORD

THÉRÈSE KUOH-MOUKOURY

With the symbolic art of embroidery and sewing at her fingertips, Awu is a living portrait of an Africa exuding talent and finesse, forging ahead without hesitation. Through the lives of her characters in a village on the edge of the tropical forest, Justine Mintsa also conveys to her readers, however, the realities of the continent where despite great strides in development, dysfunction within society still exists.

Today's Gabonese woman is modern and progressive even if she still remains somewhat attached to traditional values. One can easily find her even in this rural area where *Awu's Story* takes place, this contemporary African woman whose aim is to actively participate in the evolution and modernization of her country. Her prime objective is evident; she is on an individual and collective quest to attain the best living conditions possible. She seeks wealth, but she also has aspirations of living a moral life in a world that is just.

Steering clear of hostility and theoretical discourse alike, Mintsa's fictitious heroine, Awu, much like any woman in real life, is concerned with practicalities. She challenges injustice, but more importantly perhaps, she adopts alternative solutions in order to combat the horrifying customs that are incompatible with the realities of today's world.

In both her private and professional worlds, Awu offers intelligence, sanity, and generosity in opposition to tyranny, cruelty, and corruption. Through her courage and her thoroughly African ingenuity, Awu contributes to the emergence of a new kind of humanism for the twenty-first century. In spite of overwhelming bureaucracy and its consequences that prove even more damaging for those residing outside urban areas on the African continent, Awu's sense of dignity, morality, and justice remains intact. She condemns social abuses of any kind and abhors the fact that certain sectors of society are unable to move ahead. She denounces tribalism but also the idolatry of politics.

A novel about the realities of rural living, but also a story about daily existence, *Awu's Story* is both a cry for justice and the song of a human soul.

TRANSLATOR'S NOTE

This project was supported in part through an ACES + Opportunity Grant awarded through Case Western Reserve University.

I wish to extend my thanks to Monique Le Blanche for her insights on various excerpts of the translation, and I am also grateful to Thérèse Kuoh-Moukoury, the first woman novelist of sub-Saharan Africa, for her interest in Justine Mintsa's work and for agreeing to provide the preface. Lastly, I am especially thankful to Justine Mintsa for all of her support; our long conversations in Libreville and Paris will always remain in my memory and have only reinforced my love for this particular work.

INTRODUCTION

CHERYL TOMAN

Although soft-spoken and gentle, Justine Mintsa is also an individual who exudes strength, passion, and vibrancy, much like the protagonist she created for *Awu's Story*. By nature Mintsa is humble, but the reality is that she is an author who is larger than life, and the impact she has made on African literature and the attention she has gained internationally throughout the years is unmistakable. In her home country of Gabon, Mintsa is revered as an icon and serves as a mentor and role model for a new and extremely dynamic generation of writers. Mintsa works tirelessly to promote her country's literature, discussing not only her own works but also supporting the writings of her fellow authors throughout the country. A deep appreciation for Mintsa and her efforts is evident each time she meets with her fellow citizens, young and old, for what has become over the years a multitude of events highlighting literature throughout Gabon. Most notably, Mintsa's career has produced four well-received novels: *Un seul tournant: Makôsu* (1994), *Premières lectures* (1997), *Histoire d'Awu* (2000), and *Larmes de cendre* (2010). While each text is beautifully written and unique in its contribution to African literature, it is *Histoire d'Awu* or *Awu's Story* that is considered by many as Mintsa's masterpiece.

Although Angèle Rawiri preceded her as Gabon's first woman novelist, Mintsa nonetheless enjoys a "first" of her very own; she became the first African woman writer ever to publish a novel with the prestigious publisher, Gallimard, in Paris.[1] *Histoire d'Awu* was just one of five works chosen to inaugurate the press's Continents Noirs series in 2000. Among the over one hundred works and nearly fifty authors featured throughout the years, the novel is still among the five best-selling titles of all time for the series.[2]

It was during a visit to Francophone Africa in January 1999 that Gallimard's Antoine Gallimard and Jean-Noël Schifano were inspired to create the Continents Noirs series with a mission to highlight the richness and diversity of Francophone literature of the African continent and its diaspora. With its exceptional literary merit and originality, Mintsa's novel was chosen to inaugurate the series, although Mintsa still recalls the day when she nervously sent the manuscript to Gallimard from the bustling Central Post Office in Libreville. Upon receiving Gallimard's letter indicating the acceptance of her manuscript for publication, Mintsa did not open the envelope immediately out of fear of rejection.[3] Quite to the contrary, *Histoire d'Awu* was embraced not only by its publisher, but also quickly received international acclaim and was later adapted for theater by Michel Ndaot and performed to a packed house at the Centre Culturel Français in Libreville on November 9, 2006.[4] Eighteen years after it was first published in the original French, the novel continues to collect accolades, and it is most appropriate that the first translation of the novel into English—*Awu's Story*—is now becoming part of the long-standing French Voices collection featuring prominent African literature in translation published by the University of Nebraska Press.

MINTSA'S OWN STORY AND JOURNEY AS A WRITER

Justine Mintsa was born on September 8, 1949, in Oyem, a town in the north of Gabon that is heavily populated by the Fang ethnic group. She is the third child of twelve siblings. At the time of her birth, Mintsa's father was an elementary school teacher and her mother had received her education at the *école ménagère* in home economics, as was popular in the United States at the time as well for women of that generation. Mintsa's Protestant upbringing served not only as a source of spiritual inspiration, but also guided her education and cultivated her passion for writing and reading. The first years of her schooling were spent at the Mission Protestante de Mfoul in Oyem.

After serving as a chief administrator of national education in his country, Mintsa's father eventually became Gabon's second ambassador to France, enrolling his daughter at the Lycée Molière in Paris once she had finished middle school in Gabon. She completed half of her secondary school studies in Paris but returned to Gabon to pass her *baccalauréat*, the culminating competitive examination marking the end of high school in the French education system that Gabon had inherited. She spent her first two years of post-secondary study at Gabon's only university at the time, Université Nationale du Gabon (now known as Omar Bongo University), where she majored in Spanish and British literature. She was eventually awarded a scholarship to continue her studies in London and then was admitted to universities in Great Britain and France before eventually earning her doctorate in English literature at the Université de Rouen at the end of 1977.

After her graduate studies, Mintsa married. Her husband, a professor of physics and chemistry, was appointed to oversee the opening in Franceville of Gabon's second national university, the Masuku campus for science and technology. Mintsa accompanied her husband in that venture as they raised their family there while pursuing their respective academic careers. Having already developed an avid interest in writing as a child, Mintsa continued to write but merely for pleasure; she explains that it was never her intention early on to publish her work. However, it was the loss of her son in a car accident—a traumatic event which for her is still impossible to talk about to this day—that pushed her to publish her first novel, *Un seul tournant: Makôsu*. The novel became a way of recounting the tragedy to others without having to talk about it herself, a means through which others could learn what she and her family had lived that would release her from the overwhelming burden of recalling the event again and again. Writing *Makôsu* was more than therapeutic for Mintsa. She stated in a 2015 interview in Libreville: "If I hadn't [written it], I wouldn't have survived."[5]

Mintsa and her family eventually returned to Libreville, and she continued in her position at Omar Bongo University as an English professor at the Faculty of Letters and Human Sciences. She became a dynamic member of the English department, directing an English language scholarly journal entitled WAVES and creating a theater troupe known as Wolespeare Company, a hybrid name paying tribute to both the Nobel Prize laureate from Nigeria, Wole Soyinka, and to William Shakespeare. Mintsa wrote several plays in English for the theater troupe but they were never published. The troupe was successful for six years, and Mintsa was proud of the Anglophone element that the project brought to the Faculty of Arts. However, nonending strikes plaguing the entire educational system in Gabon were taxing; general unrest, impossible working conditions, and a lack of infrastructure in the country at that time were the ultimate causes of the troupe's demise.

Mintsa had begun her academic career in 1978 as a teaching assistant in English, and one year later she was named chair of the department. She remained at the university until her retirement from academia in 2014.

Mintsa often took on simultaneous duties, including five years (1997–2001) as president of the Union des Écrivains Gabonais, also known as UDEG, an organization that was made up of over fifty published authors in Gabon at that time. UDEG is and always has been extremely active in promoting and distributing the publications of Gabonese authors in spite of the unique challenges publishing on the African continent entails. Similar to her father's career path, Mintsa was appointed director of culture in Gabon's Ministry of Culture and Arts from 2000 until 2009.[6] From 2012 until her general retirement in 2016, she was the advisor to Gabon's prime minister as head of the Department of Culture, Education, Youth and Sports.[7] While assuming these concurrent positions may have seemed impossible and even incompatible to some, Mintsa had always viewed them to be roles that were complementary. Indeed, she coordinated them remarkably well, and they enabled her to become an advocate and an ambassador of sorts for the promotion of Gabonese literature and women's writing. Her work within the Ministry of Culture and Education allowed her to direct projects that enhanced museums and theaters throughout the country in addition to pursuing initiatives in Gabonese art and culture in general. Through these and other professional activities, Mintsa continued to write and publish. *Histoire d'Awu* was preceded by a novel for children entitled *Premières lectures* (1997), a text still widely read and discussed today in schools across Gabon.

In 1999 Gallimard discovered Mintsa and her manuscript, which she had originally entitled *La pension*, a direct reference to the elusive retirement that is ultimately responsible for taking the life of Obame Afane at the end of the novel. Mintsa had written the work as a tribute to her father's friend who had been killed in a road accident traveling from Oyem to Libreville, where he was headed to file documents for his retirement. In writing her narrative Mintsa reasoned that her father's friend must have been married, and so she created his wife, the character known as Awu. According to Mintsa, Gallimard questioned the title, *La pension*, indicating that they thought it was not about the retirement pension at all: "C'est l'histoire d'Awu" ("This is Awu's story"). So the title was then determined in a most definitive way and Awu became its star. This was eye-opening for Mintsa, who had not initially realized the impact that Awu would have on her readers. She claimed her first reaction to Gallimard's suggestion of a change in title was: "Oh no, Obame has been killed a second time." However, Mintsa is far from displeased at the thought that Awu may inspire her readers a bit more than her husband, Obame Afane.

After *Histoire d'Awu* was published in 2000, Mintsa was invited across the globe to promote the novel, and she received numerous honors at home and abroad while continuing her many responsibilities in Gabon. She also produced works of scholarly writing, the most significant being a work in cultural studies on traditional marriages entitled *Protocole du mariage au Gabon* (2003) that she coauthored with Grégory Ngbwa Mintsa. Admittedly, her professional duties limited the time she had available for creative writing, which explains the three-year hiatus from the ministry that she took in order to finish her fourth novel, *Larmes de cendre*, that appeared at the end of 2010. Mintsa originally published *Larmes* with Éditions Tira in Béjaïa, Algeria, although its second printing in 2012 is with L'Harmattan in Paris. Mintsa was impressed with Tira and its editor, whom she had met during a visit to Algeria to promote *Histoire d'Awu*. She then decided to publish the first edition of *Larmes* with Tira as a gesture of support for publishers on the African continent and also as a means of diversifying her audience. Ironically, Mintsa has been criticized for such showings of support after her success at Gallimard,[8] but such efforts to promote culture and reading at all levels of society have always been essential to Mintsa.

Despite her fame and numerous honors, it is not at all uncommon for Mintsa to accept invitations to elementary and secondary schools in Gabon to discuss her works with children and adolescents. In 1997 Mintsa initiated a project known as the *caravane littéraire* (literary caravan) where she and other writers of UDEG embarked on a remarkable 4 × 4 journey to the most remote corners of the country to ensure for themselves not only the distribution of Gabonese literature in schools but also the inclusion of these works in the national education program. The caravan project attracted the attention of Paulette Missambo, who was then Gabon's minister of national education at the time. Missambo asked the caravan to make a stop at the Institut Pédagogique National (National Pedagogical Institute) in order to drop off titles that should be included on the nationwide reading list for students. Thanks to the caravan, these suggested works officially became part of the education system the following year in 1998—the first time in the history of Gabon that its own literary works were to be officially taught in schools across the country. Mintsa considers this moment to be a victory of a lifetime. If today we witness several young writers in Gabon such as Edna Merey-Apinda, who continue to initiate similar projects with Gabonese schoolchildren across the country, it is in part thanks to Mintsa's original caravan that has served as inspiration.[9]

Now in the early years of retirement from her professional life, Justine Mintsa is looking forward to completing several writing projects already in progress, although her four novels have already left an indelible mark on African literature; she is an author who undeniably is an important figure in Gabonese literary history. As Gabon is a country whose literature is already enjoying unique distinctions and whose women writers have far surpassed the overall productivity of their peers in other African nations, Mintsa's accomplishments are no small feat. Her illustrious career thus far suggests that we have not heard the last from Justine Mintsa, and it is expected that she will continue to enrich the literary scene.

AWU'S STORY: A SIGNIFICANT WORK

Although Gabon's people are diverse, the Fang ethnic group makes up nearly forty percent of the country's total population and is found in significant numbers in neighboring countries.[10] One original element of Mintsa's writing that is especially true for *Awu's Story* is how this author integrates aspects of the Fang language, culture, and oral traditions into the contemporary novel. This technique only adds to its richness, however, and is not meant to alienate readers in any way: it is nonetheless Mintsa's way of "decolonizing" the novel written in French.[11] Thus, Mintsa can be considered not only a Gabonese author but also a writer of the Fang diaspora.

Interestingly, there are many words, symbols, and references in *Awu's Story* that may escape a reader who is completely unfamiliar with the Fang language and culture, but this hidden layer of meaning is actually one of the most brilliant aspects of the work. While *Awu's Story* is easily understood by anyone regardless of culture or background, it nonetheless holds a myriad of treasures for readers in the know. This additional layer of meaning, although hidden for some, potentially provides a much more evocative read than initially thought. It can even be said that while *Awu's Story* addresses a wide audience, the extra layer of meaning serves as Mintsa's unique gift to her Fang readers not only in Gabon but also to those in the region and of the diaspora.

In fact, one has to go no further than the title and the name of the novel's star protagonist to start unlocking some of the hidden elements of this work. The word *awu* in the Fang language means "death," and it is the shortened form of the character's full name, Awudabiran', which translates as "death disturbs" or even "death, it destroys."[12] This detail imbues the title of the novel with a new layer of meaning; this is not only Awu's story, referring to the protagonist, but it is also a story that revolves around death.

Admittedly the novel does touch upon the subject of death quite often, commencing with the death of Bella, the beloved first wife of Obame Afane who, unable to bear a child, dies of a broken heart the moment Awu and Obame's twins are born (33). Next, Obame's sister, Akut, declares the symbolic death of her daughter, Ada, who becomes pregnant at the age of twelve while away at boarding school (47). There is, of course, Obame Afane's own death in a bus accident as he is travelling to the capital to straighten out his long-awaited pension (97), and finally, Awu clearly threatens to kill Nguema (Obame Afane's brother who has inherited Awu according to custom) if he dares to touch her (109).

True to the meaning conveyed through the phrase *Awudabiran'* in Fang, death undoubtedly disturbs the lives of many individuals in the novel. However, upon realizing the meaning behind Awu's name, the reader may be confused as to why this endearing character has a name with such an apparently dark meaning. Mintsa has placed the Fang ritual pertaining to widows at the center not only of *Awu's Story* but also of her latest novel, *Larmes de cendre*, thereby joining other African women writers, most notably Cameroonian playwright Werewere Liking, who have also introduced similar rituals in their works. In Liking's play, *The Power of Um* (1996), the protagonist Ngond Libii also rebels against the harsh treatment of widows in her own Bassa society. Awu, Biloa, and Ngond Libii are all examples of protagonists who have been ritually silenced; what is gained through their rebellion in their respective situations is indeed something positive that has resulted from otherwise tragic circumstances. It is important to realize that these African rituals taking place after the death of a spouse also designate a period of atonement; death has upset the order, and the ritual is the society's attempt to reflect and analyze what has gone wrong to bring about such misfortune. The ritual becomes a way that the spirit of the deceased is appeased, a requirement if the members of the community hope to rebuild and continue on in harmony with one another. This is the positive aspect of the meaning embedded in Awu's name; her actions work to make her society better and more just for all.

In addition to highlighting certain Fang customs such as the widow's ritual, Mintsa has also rewritten examples of Fang oral literature. These contemporary versions, too, are perhaps hidden to the reader unfamiliar with Fang culture, symbols, and legends, but the lack of knowledge of such references does not render the narrative less coherent.

Although the published novel arrived relatively late in Gabon, literature had certainly not; all of Gabon's ethnic groups have rich oral traditions and sophisticated epic poetry that have been the subject of many academic and artistic studies. The Fang epic poetry known as the *mvet* is no exception and, in fact, remains some of the most widely studied and respected oral literature among Africanist scholars. The origins of the Fang people are the fabric of the mvet, and it is believed that the original leader of the Fang was a wise, fifteenth-century warrior known as Oyono Ada Ngone, who had led his people from north to south. At one point in his journey, he was severely wounded and left unconscious. His people remained loyal to him, however, and never abandoned him. When Oyono Ada Ngone awoke, he related to his people how he had been visited in his unconscious state by a divine spirit who taught him how to create an instrument that would be the tool for educating his people and calling them to action (Nguimbi 2012, 144). This is generally believed by the Fang to be the origin of the mvet, the name that refers to the epic poetry as well as to the musical instrument used in its performance.

In his brilliant essay entitled "De la mort du maître à la mort symbolique de l'école: pour une pratique stylistique dans *Histoire d'Awu* de Justine Mintsa," Arnold Nguimbi relates how Mintsa has rewritten the fifteenth-century hero and founder of the Fang as Obame Afane in *Awu's Story*. This is a significant detail because the mvet is typically an art form that is interpreted exclusively by men. Presenting us with her contemporary version of the epic is Mintsa's way of paying tribute to it, but doing so as a woman writer may also be seen as a defiance of the male-dominated aspect of the tradition. Mintsa is therefore sending a strong message that women need to appropriate the epic before such traditions are lost forever. Mintsa clearly believes that women are as responsible as men for preserving traditions worth keeping. Mintsa's contemporary rewrite of the mvet offers a less violent version than the original, replacing the warrior's weapon with a more useful one for Obame Afane, the schoolteacher—a writing utensil: "In his right hand, Obame Afane, the son, held a stylus, the weapon of his time" (105).

There are yet other ways that Fang oral literature has inspired *Awu's Story*. Throughout the novel, the reader notes the importance of the local river; Obame Afane and his family go there to swim, but more importantly to become reenergized both physically and mentally. For Obame, this river became a place where he "surrendered his body to the whims of the water" (41). Having been born on its banks, Obame had such an intimate relationship with the river that Awu was almost jealous of it (41). His morning routine included swimming there every morning before teaching his students, but he also went there to muster up the strength and wisdom needed to confront exceptional circumstances in his life, such as the meeting of the elders that he had to lead to decide the fate of his pregnant twelve-year-old niece.

Of course, water is a universal symbol of life and rebirth, but it is interesting to explore the probable connection between the Fang and the river in *Awu's Story*. Among the oral tales of the Fang, there is an origin myth that speaks of Ndabiare, the woman recognized as the founder of the first Fang village. In his work about the history of the Fang, Mba Abessole notes that the expectation is that women will transmit the values of Fang culture and the history of its people.

This role comes directly from the aforementioned origin myth, adding another empowering aspect to motherhood which does not exist in the same way in Western cultures (Mba Abessole 2006, 10). Even though men may ultimately be regarded as superior to women in Fang culture (Ngou 2007, 225), the Fang woman's obligation to her community cannot be understated. As fellow Fang and Gabonese writer Honorine Ngou notes, a new bride is often given the name *ndâ ngoura*—literally, "the entire house" (Ngou 2007, 170), or *midzâ* "the pillar of the village" (Ngou 2007, 231)—and indeed there are references in *Awu's Story* that both Awu and Bella had become pillars of the village upon their marriage to Obame Afane (34 and 32).

So considering this cultural context, it is interesting to analyze both the importance of this origin myth that places women at the center of society and Obame Afane's relationship with the river. In the original tale, Ndabiare is alone when she gives birth, just as Obame's mother is for a time until her mother-in-law is able to join and assist her. Ndabiare gives birth to two "children"—one human and one egg (Mba Abessole 2006, 9), and immediately has a vision that her human son will become a great leader of his people. Ndabiare walks with her newborn children until she comes to a body of water, where she decides to settle for good. She keeps her human son with her on land and tosses her egg-son into the river, always keeping an eye out on the water as a way of looking after him (Mba Abessole 2006, 10). Both water and egg are strong symbols of life, and in this context they are linked to the hope for the longevity of the Fang people.

In *Awu's Story* we find a rewriting of this original myth within the narration of the birth of Obame Afane; it is not Mintsa's intention, however, to stray too far from the symbols, beliefs, and general core message present in the original myth. The story of Obame's own birth next to the river is essential to the novel as this event coincides with the building of the first school in the village. Thus, Obame's greatness as a leader in education has already been determined at birth. His arrival into the world also signals the coming of change and new-found values generated by a society in transition. Obame as the ultimate educator is the antithesis of his colleagues at Ada's school, who are accountable for the sexual abuse of their students.

However, the similarity of the two aforementioned tales is not limited to the prediction that the respective newborn sons will grow up to be leaders of their people, nor to the proximity and importance of the river. Although the egg is absent in Mintsa's rewrite, there are equivalent symbols of life in *Awu's Story*. Mintsa quite often refers to the "Nourishing Mass" (her term for the umbilical cord) and the "Mass of Life" (the placenta). The capitalization of these terms merely emphasizes Mintsa's personification of them and indeed, the fact that they are "throbbing" (43) suggests they have a life of their own, or at least a relevant energy. If Ndabiare's tossing of her egg-son into the river may seem mysterious, Mintsa's rewrite may actually aid the reader in interpreting the meaning of that action. In *Awu's Story* Obame's grandmother buries both the Mass of Life and the Nourishing Mass in a hole dug with the help of an almost regal machete that had severed Obame from his mother. Mintsa writes: "The Mass of Life saw the light of day one last time before taking up residence in its new womb: that of the earth—this same earth that it would also rejuvenate" (44). The Mass of Life clearly had a new mission: "to fertilize and impregnate the earth, to itself produce in order to sustain the life of men and women who were themselves called upon to perpetuate the lineage" (44).

Thus, these universal symbols of life—egg, water, earth, umbilical cord, and placenta—all serve the same purpose in the Fang origin myth as well as in Mintsa's retelling of it. The egg becomes one with the water just as the Mass of Life is protected by the earth surrounding it. Since Obame has deep connections with these symbols his entire life, it is no longer a mystery why the river gives him undeniable strength as he swims in it. After reading this beautiful segment in the novel, the reader is all the more shocked and affected by the horrific conditions in which Ada gives birth in the provincial hospital, where any water present is tainted with the blood of dozens of previous patients, and the magnificent machete has been replaced by a rusty razor blade (67). Even the "Mass of Life" has been reduced here to a mere "mass of flesh" (67).

Recounting these fascinating and striking aspects of Fang culture is Mintsa's way of disorienting the reader a bit, causing him or her to question if Westernization and urbanization necessarily lead to development and a more modern society. At one point after Ada gives birth, Awu is standing bewildered outside the hospital, holding a bloodied steel tray containing the placenta. An elderly woman nearby senses that Awu has lost her bearings and has no idea what to do next. She reminds Awu, however, that "this Mass of Life must fertilize the city" (71), which conveys a highly symbolic message—positive aspects of tradition must remain to nourish contemporary society and to ultimately drive its progress. While other African authors may also express similar messages in their texts, few do so as eloquently as Mintsa has done in *Awu's Story*.

A SUMMARY OF MINTSA'S OTHER LITERARY WORKS

Histoire d'Awu was not Mintsa's first novel, even though it was the one that has brought her the most critical acclaim. First published in 1994, *Un seul tournant: Makôsu* marks Mintsa's first official venture into literature. The first edition of *Makôsu* was published by La Pensée Universelle in Paris, but was republished in 2004 by L'Harmattan, also in Paris, leading to confusion in some literary sources on the original publication date of the novel. This common and recurring mistake leads one to believe that *Premières lectures* (1997) was actually Mintsa's first novel.

Mintsa rarely refers to Gabon directly in her works, preferring instead to plunge the reader into the everyday life of a fictional African country in order to take on issues that are pertinent to the continent as a whole. In this particular novel, the setting is a university campus named Makôsu in a city called Falaville located in the country of Govan. There is no doubt of the reference—the Masuku campus, better known as the University of Science and Technology in Franceville.

Mintsa's husband, who had a significant administrative role at the new campus, is clearly the inspiration for the vice-chancellor in the novel.

Knowing how Mintsa subsequently lived the tragic event and its aftermath that all led to the creation of this novel, one understands more readily the style in which *Makôsu* was written. The novel begins with a letter entirely in English to a friend and assumed former colleague living in the United States. There is no translation of this letter that nonetheless provides the context for the entire novel, but there are sufficient details and footnotes throughout the text that make up for any disadvantage a non-English-speaking reader may have in the beginning. The letter is actually an introduction to a series of diary entries recounting to the friend the events of the narrator's personal and professional life of the past five years. Thus, *Makôsu* is both an epistolary novel and an example of narrative journalism, but there are yet other elements that make its style even more unique.

The first part of *Makôsu* essentially recounts the founding of the university and describes the special challenges of doing so in a developing country. The novel also shows how much of a role that France, the former colonizer of "Govan," still plays in the country, and while some assistance is appreciated and even necessary in the building of the university, the text provides a unique perspective and commentary about the lingering effects of colonialism and neocolonialism and the struggle of former colonies to become truly independent from France.

The first part ends with the mention of a well-deserved family vacation by 4 × 4 vehicle in the surrounding region that the family has yet to discover because of their heavy workload (41). This is followed by a two-page poetic text that marks an abrupt break in the diary entries which, of course, is highly symbolic of the upset that the family lives as a result of the road accident that claims the life of the couple's child, one of their twins: "Six of us came back, that very same morning, from the road to Ogonza / Five dazed souls and a lifeless body" (42).[13] Incredible sadness and anger abound in these two pages of powerful text that use relatively few words but unmistakably demonstrate Mintsa's enormous talent as a writer.

The narrative then picks up once again with poignant journal entries describing the tragedy in more detail and revealing insights into customs and beliefs surrounding death in various African societies. Some believe that death never happens just by chance, and this belief leads certain family members in the novel to suspect that somehow the couple has "sacrificed" the deceased child to ensure their own success (46). This leaves the couple outraged, and the reader is then a witness to a subsequent purification ritual (also common after the death of a family member) allowing the family to move on from the tragedy (48).

The novel's focus once again turns to the university in the following parts (identified as "Second Year," "Third Year," etc.), this time emphasizing political unrest and strikes that plague the campus and the country. The narration allows the reader to realize how individuals and families are personally affected by such challenging working conditions and the general atmosphere. Mintsa continues to pepper her prose with short poetic verses throughout, and this is her way of respecting her art as a creative writer; the novel may have been far less powerful if it had relied only on historical facts about the university's beginnings.

Mintsa often refers to major world issues of the late 1980s, such as the fall of the Berlin Wall and the overturning of the Ceauşescu regime in Romania (108), which allow the reader to interpret the events in *Makôsu* from a different perspective. Mintsa does not miss an opportunity to relate the newly found freedom associated with the fall of communism in Europe with the restrictions and separation Africans face due to the reality of colonial borders: "Their dream is a reality. I know that my own is impossible. I have relatives in all of the neighboring countries. Because of these blindly drawn borders, they are all now considered foreigners" (108).

With an obvious reference to her own Fang ethnic group spread out over Gabon, Cameroon, Equatorial Guinea, and Congo, Mintsa allows her readers to realize the emotional toll that colonialism continues to have on African families. However, Mintsa also cites the liberation of Nelson Mandela (110) and the independence of Namibia (115), which both occurred in 1990, providing a glimmer of hope for Mintsa's "impossible dream." She nonetheless remains realistic: "Africa is entirely free, yes, but being independent doesn't mean that it is free from domination; while this domination may no longer be political, it is certainly economic" (115).

At the very end of the fourth part of the novel, Mintsa integrates an important moment in Gabonese history into *Makôsu*, that of Gabon's 1991 adoption of a multiparty system of government (116). Although this borrowed event is meant to mark a hopeful period in the novel, the university and Govan are wracked by turmoil that presents challenges for the establishment of real democracy in the country. The unionization of university faculty has the full support of students, and subsequent hostile interactions with the Govanese prime minister create a situation that puts the entire academic year at risk. The novel ends on this uncertain note, with the cancellation of the rest of the school year in early May with, at best, a tentative return to classes scheduled for the fall (140).

Perhaps Mintsa's first novel did not gain as much attention as her subsequent ones only because the rather specific context of the African university may be less relatable for some as opposed to more universal subjects such as friendships and marriages presented in each of her other works. Nonetheless, *Makôsu* captures raw and authentic emotions on many levels through the interweaving of fiction and nonfiction and prose and poetry. The novel is arguably of historical value as well for its compilation of facts surrounding a very tumultuous period in contemporary Gabonese history. For these reasons alone, it is a work deserving of further critical attention.

Yet another novel that appeared before *Histoire d'Awu* is *Premières lectures* (1997), a work still widely read today. Although it is well-received by upper-elementary-school students, *Premières lectures* is enjoyable and instructive for readers of any age. The story takes place in a village seemingly untouched by Western influence, but the arrival of Brian, a teenage British traveler, reminds us all that change is inevitable. Brian's presence is not threatening, however, and it is significant that he also is perceived as a child. His interactions with Obone, the fifteen-year-old daughter of a village elder, reflect the open-mindedness of youth, as the two have heartfelt and enlightening exchanges that stop short of a romantic relationship, a clear message to Mintsa's young readers to complete one's education before dabbling in affairs of the heart.

Obone is, in fact, the narrator of the novel, and this choice is clearly meant to empower Mintsa's young female protagonist. In fact, Obone fairs much better than Brian, her counterpart, since she can speak her own native language plus French, two languages that are completely inaccessible to Brian. Obone states: "Even in my wildest dreams, I couldn't imagine that I, a young black girl, could speak French better than a white boy! I had to face the facts: I was more skilled than a white! I was more skilled than a man! I was superior to the white man!" (22).

Of course, there is the suggestion that Brian, as an English speaker, ultimately does not need to learn Obone's native language (nor even French, for that matter) in order to succeed, whereas Obone absolutely needs to rely on her knowledge of French to advance in life. However, Mintsa uses the metaphor of blindness to address the subject of race and race relations in the novel. Obone's father, the village elder, is already physically blind, but this allows him to be more accepting of the British traveler (18–19) because race is a social construct that relies on what is seen. Brian's blindness, however, is due to privilege—as a male and as a Westerner—and although ultimately his future will not be threatened because of his lack of knowledge of African languages or French, he is still shut out from the richness of Obone's grandfather's stories that he tells each night to other villagers.

Without diminishing any character or way of life, *Premières lectures* manages to teach children the realities of racism and inequality in today's world and encourages them to fight against it while maintaining an open mind. Thus, this particular novel embraces multiculturalism but cautions against "blindness" of all forms. The village is portrayed authentically and shown in a positive light—a detail likely to provoke lively debate among urban dwellers, schoolchildren included. African literature for children is not yet very abundant, and thus *Premières lectures* joins other celebrated examples of children's literature brought to the forefront by major African authors such as Ivorian writer Véronique Tadjo. Since Mintsa's publication of *Premières lectures*, several works for children written by Gabon's second generation of writers have also emerged, including Edna Merey-Apinda's *Les aventures d'Imya, petite fille du Gabon* (2004) and other texts geared more toward adolescents such as Alice Endamne's *C'est demain qu'on s'fait la malle* (2008). Thus Mintsa's second novel has had much more of an impact on Gabonese society than its mere forty-one pages initially suggest.

In addition to the two novels that precede *Histoire d'Awu*, Mintsa's fourth novel, *Larmes de cendre* (2010), is also worthy of note and is the work that is the most similar to Mintsa's masterpiece. In *Awu's Story*, Mintsa alludes to the fact that what is most harmful about a custom is not necessarily the custom itself but rather how it can be manipulated by individuals in order to gain power. This is the main premise behind *Larmes*. The Fang ritual applying to widows is ever present in Mintsa's most recent novel, but the violence of it is heightened here. For Awu, the particular cruelty of the ritual as it was carried out by her sister-in-law Akut is just one of several hardships and obstacles for her to overcome. In *Larmes*, however, the life of the main character, Biloa, is completely shattered because of the ritual, and this ultimately becomes the indirect cause of the protagonist's death.

In *Larmes* the reader is introduced to Kan, a young doctor and enthusiastic painter who is first attracted to Biloa when he runs into her at the airport. After this initial encounter he cannot stop thinking about her, and he thus devotes his time to painting her portrait. Several months pass until Kan realizes that his father, who is an attorney, is representing a rape victim—a widow who was violated during the ritual of atonement. This client is none other than Biloa.

The same woman who was stunningly beautiful and full of life at the airport some months prior is now a shadow of her former self; she is unable to speak and severely traumatized—a "body without a soul" (83). Biloa is brought to Kan's medical office by Cécile, the very sister who is among those responsible for arranging the brutal rape during the ritual. However, Cécile is at first unaware that it is actually Kan's father who is representing Biloa. Kan prescribes art therapy and gardening to aid Biloa in the healing process. Her condition eventually improves, and after several years Kan and Biloa fall in love and marry. Biloa, however, refuses a traditional ceremony in light of what has already happened to her in the name of tradition. Both sides of the family are less than pleased with this marriage for a variety of reasons, and this merely complicates matters for Biloa.

The reader eventually learns that revenge is behind the extreme brutality of the widow ritual for Biloa's apparent violation of the *akagha*, a Fang word roughly translated as "an order handed down by the gods."[14] In this particular case the akagha was initiated by Biloa's childless aunt. It ensured that the daughters in the family would be powerful and of high social standing, but they were prohibited from marrying or having children without risking their own death (21). Cécile willingly accepts this fate, but Biloa categorically rejects it by marrying her first husband, who eventually becomes ill and dies in the beginning of the novel. In fact, Biloa dares to defy the akagha yet again not only by her new marriage to Kan but also by the couple's decision to have a child; the prophecy of the akagha indeed manifests itself as Biloa dies just hours after giving birth to the couple's daughter (129). As the couple never had a traditional marriage, Kan's right to claim his wife's body for burial is denied until he pays what can be perceived as a ransom. He refuses to do so solely on the grounds that those manipulating the tradition would triumph, and he believes this would be a sign of disrespect for Biloa, who loathed such dark aspects of prevailing customs. Completely defeated, Kan utters: "This tradition has finally caught up with us" (137). But Cécile does not emerge as a winner either; by the end of the novel, she loses her job and the wealth and status that comes with it and is eventually admitted to a psychiatric hospital.

Perhaps it is Biloa's commentary on the manipulation of tradition that will be difficult for Mintsa's readers to forget: "I would be lucky if I lived in a country where tradition is not a weapon of intimidation that obliges people who are respectful of their culture to serve the interests of the unscrupulous, calculating people of the lowest kind. For me, true luck is to enjoy freedom while showing respect for the other" (114).

The fact that Mintsa addresses age-old traditions, conveys ideas handed down through Fang oral literature, and accords the village an important place in her works sometimes leads critics to believe that she is not writing about contemporary issues. But as Fortunat Obiang Essono explains: "Modernity in the work of Justine Mintsa comes through in the expression of concern and disillusionment over the post-colonial world, prisoner of its own contradictions between progress and decline, novelty and archaism (2006, 163)." In this sense, Mintsa is very much an author writing about the contradictions facing African countries today as Africans attempt to define and shape for themselves what their own societies should look like.

A NOVEL DEFYING "INVISIBILITY"

Gabon is an exception in the history of literature; it is the only country worldwide whose first novelist was female. Although oral tradition in Gabon is centuries old, Angèle Rawiri is credited for having published the first novel in the country, her 1980 work entitled *Elonga*. Admittedly, the novel arrived late in Gabon compared to other countries on the African continent and beyond, but nonetheless it is revealing that this significant fact about Gabon's first novelist is not widely known, not even among literary scholars. Indeed, Gabon's literary production since the publication of Rawiri's landmark novel is quite simply astonishing. While it is normal for a given country to have decades with stronger literary production than others, Gabon's writers, once they had started, have never stopped. Furthermore, most of the first generation of women writers are still publishing, although now there is a young and vibrant second generation that have added their voices as well. Of course, the country also boasts many male authors. However, by 2011, the president of the Union des Écrivains Gabonais at the time, Sylvie Ntsame, had already noted that half of Gabon's published writers were women, and that number has only increased to surpass the number of male writers in the country today (Toman 2016, xv).

There are other realities worthy of note that show the predominance of women writers in Gabon. Of course, Justine Mintsa was the first female African author to publish her novel, *Histoire d'Awu*, with Gallimard in Paris, but she is also considered the second female novelist in Gabon after Rawiri. Moreover, women writers such as Chantal Magalie Mbazoo Kassa and Sylvie Ntsame founded some of the very first publishing houses on the African continent, La Maison Gabonaise du Livre and Éditions Ntsame, respectively. Similarly, novelist Nadia Origo had her own innovative idea when launching La Doxa Éditions in Paris in 2010, with a mission of providing African writers the opportunity to have their writings with a focus on social justice published in Europe without the need to tailor their works for a specifically European audience. Most recently in June 2016, Edna Merey-Apinda, who lives in Gabon's economic capital of Port-Gentil, created the very first virtual bookstore in the country. This bookstore, known as La Bonne Page, operates from wherever the author has her computer and has no physical premises; nonetheless, it is incredibly successful in distributing Gabonese literature and numerous other titles to those who might not have access to it otherwise.[15]

Despite the noteworthy accomplishments of its women writers, Gabonese literature remained almost inexplicably invisible until only recently. Ironically, the very reason for its uniqueness was the probable cause of its invisibility—the fact that women are at the forefront. The acclaimed literary critic Irène Assiba d'Almeida has spoken famously of an "empty canon" in African Francophone literature, and the careers of the continent's women writers have been affected by this the most.

The empty canon acknowledges that actual literary works exist, but they have remained "unknown, unpraised, uncriticized" because no one bothered to look at them (d'Almeida 2009, xxii). Of course, Gabonese women writers are not the only ones who have historically found themselves in the empty canon; female authors have consistently been overlooked universally for the simple reason that in a patriarchal society, a man's words are generally considered more valid and more important than a woman's. Cameroonian Thérèse Kuoh-Moukoury, the first woman novelist of sub-Saharan Africa, had finished her manuscript for *Rencontres essentielles* in 1956 but did not find a publisher until 1969—some fifteen years after her male counterparts such as Mongo Beti and Ferdinand Oyono had already found publishers for their works.

Having published much later than their peers in other African nations, Gabonese women fortunately did not face similar hurdles in their own country and, in fact, their works have always been well-received at home. But the fact remains that their works were for a long time invisible to those outside of Gabon, proving how Africans often are not allowed to determine what works make up their own literary canon. However, prominent literature scholars in Gabon such as Pierre Ndemby-Mamfoumby and Pierre Claver-Mongui have over the last several years produced outstanding volumes and essays of literary criticism that have allowed the Gabonese to begin to take back their own canon from outside critics. One text that has defied the empty canon from the beginning, attracting the most critical attention both inside Gabon and out, is Justine Mintsa's *Histoire d'Awu*. Thus, this work has greatly contributed to the visibility of the country's literature overall; its English translation, entitled *Awu's Story*, promises to thrust Gabonese literature into the spotlight with a new audience of non-French-speaking readers. Although a few titles of Gabonese literature have already begun to appear in English translation, *Awu's Story* is probably the most significant considering its continued success with Gallimard since its original publication in French in 2000.

Awu's Story is ageless; at times, it reads like an ancient tale of oral literature, and indeed such narratives have served as its inspiration. However, Mintsa clearly reminds us in part two of her novel that we are indeed "at the dawn of the twenty-first century" (67). The novel's characters are entirely relatable, and Mintsa manages to convey profound emotions in a love story that is unconventional, which makes the novel all the more attractive. The story's ultimate tragedy is important and central, but it does not take away from Awu's moments of strength and hope that transform her into the unintentional hero of the novel, providing a lasting sense of optimism for the reader.

Histoire d'Awu and now its English translation, *Awu's Story*, defy the invisibility that has unfortunately plagued too many other titles of African literature; both Gabonese and non-Gabonese critics have ensured this novel a definitive place in the canon. Its continued success also elevates African women's writing in general. Furthermore, the novel's discussion of cultural references and symbols from the Fang ethnic group contributes to an African feminist discourse, which in turn has become richer lest we forget that African feminists, too, have struggled against invisibility, so often overshadowed by the Western discipline, which has not always been inclusive and appropriate. Justine Mintsa's work has definitely filled a void in this regard. Mintsa's depiction of a women's space in transition—the widow's ritual carried out exclusively by women—shows us that almost every female character in *Awu's Story* has defied tradition in some way in order to live the way in which she chooses. In fact, nearly all of the female members of Obame Afane's family are incredibly forward thinking except for Ekobekobe, described as a "sister-in-law from the village" (99) who attempts to brutalize Awu during the widow's ritual. After quickly being put in her place by Ntsame and Ada, Ekobekobe leaves the village in shame (102–3), as there is clearly no place for her in this feminine space undergoing transformation. In contrast, Obame Afane's eldest sister, Ntsame, is an extremely strong and outspoken character in the novel who also becomes Awu's best advocate. Inarguably feminist, Ntsame rejected both traditional marriage and children, going off to the city alone and associating with revolutionaries before finally coming back to the village to catch her breath a bit. Ntsame famously stands up to men and cares little about what the village thinks of her (53). Although villagers may criticize her in private, she is a woman who commands respect and knows how to assert her power when she needs to. It is clear that the young Ada will follow in her footsteps as she also stands up against the harsh treatment of her Aunt Awu, revealing at the same time the injustice of a society in which girls away at boarding school are sexually abused at the hands of their teachers and administrators with no recourse to speak of. It can even be said that the misguided Akut has also made an attempt to live her life differently than a traditional woman of the village would, but her mistake is that she was not interested in formal education early on. Thus, she does not have the tools or the respect of Ntsame to make her plan work. This is also why it is important that the young Ada return to school so that she will not end up like her mother, or else hopelessly caught in the harmful practices of tradition like Ekobekobe. Thus, it is not only through the revered schoolteacher known as Obame Afane—also named Sikolo, the Fang word for "school"—that the importance of education in the novel is conveyed. It is important to remember that Awu, too, has a diploma and was once employed as a teacher and that she continues to educate those around her until the end of the novel. African feminisms are therefore successfully asserted by educated women who have the tools necessary to reconcile contemporary and traditional practices for the good of everyone.

No reader is left indifferent after reading *Awu's Story*. Either in the original French or in English translation, the novel is arguably a classic of African literature. It is both poignant and instructive, and its characters are inspiring yet wonderfully ordinary at the same time. The text can be used as an introduction to African literature, yet it is equally fascinating to the well-seasoned reader. Mintsa is indeed a masterful writer with poetic prose that remains entirely accessible. Awu's story thus comprises a lifetime of events that leave an indelible impression on the reader, for whom the chain stitch soon takes on new meaning.

1. Author Sylvie Kandé's *Lagon, lagunes* (2000) was also among the first five titles published in Gallimard's series. However, Kandé is considered a diaspora writer, having been born in Paris to a French mother and a Senegalese father.

2. For more information on the history of the Continents Noirs series, refer to Gallimard's site at http://www.gallimard.fr/Divers/Plus-sur-la-collection/Continents-noirs/(sourcenode)/116076 or an online article from the *Nouvel Observateur* dated January 18, 2000, at http://tempsreel.nouvelobs.com/culture/20000118.OBS1345/gallimard-sort-une-collection-de-romans-africains.html.

3. Personal interview with Justine Mintsa in Libreville on January 5, 2015.

4. Also from Gabon, Michel Ndaot is an acclaimed actor, writer, musician, and director of theater and film. He is best known internationally for his roles in award-winning films such as *Le grand blanc de Lambaréné* (1995) and *L'ombre de Liberty* (2005).

5. Personal interview with Justine Mintsa in Libreville on January 5, 2015.

6. In French, Mintsa's official title was "Directrice générale de la Culture au Ministère de la Culture et des Arts."

7. In French, Mintsa's official title was "Conseiller du Premier Ministre, Chef du Département Education, Culture, Jeunesse, et Sports."

8. Writer and critic Alain Mabanckou unfairly criticized Mintsa in a now infamous April 17, 2006, blog post entitled "SOS: pays africains cherchent désespérément des écrivains." Mabanckou wrote "Pour le reste, si vous voulez mon avis, le voici: il est clair que Ludovic Obiang, auteur de nouvelles, semble le plus sérieux espoir des lettres gabonaises tandis que Justine Mintsa—auteur d'*Histoire d'Awu*, roman paru en 2000—a créé une grande déception en regressant de la collection Continents noirs de Gallimard à l'Harmattan!" ("As for the rest, if you want my opinion, here it is: it is clear that short story writer Ludovic Obiang seems to be the most serious hope for Gabonese literature, whereas Justine Mintsa [author of *Histoire d'Awu*, her novel that appeared in 2000] created much disappointment, downgrading herself from Gallimard's Continent Noirs series to L'Harmattan!")

9. Edna Merey-Apinda is considered the leader of Gabon's second generation of women writers. Born in 1975, Merey-Apinda is the author of several novels and the writer and / or editor of several collections of short stories. Some of her best known works include the collections *Ce reflet dans le miroir* (2011) and *Entre nous* (2016).

10. Many sources confirm that the Fang indeed make up forty percent of Gabon's population. One of the best sources on this ethnic group is Paul Mba Abessole's *Aux sources de la culture fang* (2006).

11. There are several linguists, such as Kwaku Gyasi, who do interesting analyses of the decolonization of the African text written in French. See Gyasi's *The Francophone African Text: Translation and the Postcolonial Experience* (2006).

12. Ovono-Mendame (2006) translates the phrase *awudabiran'* as "death disturbs" or "death destroys." If one analyzes this phrase with the help of Akomo-Zoghe's *L'art de conjuguer en fang* (2009), however, the translation is perhaps more accurately "death, it destroys."

13. All translations from cited works are mine.

14. According to Akomo-Zoghe's book *Parlons Fang* (2010), the French equivalent for the word *akagha* is "ordalie." Dictionaries define *ordalie* as "a judgment handed down by god(s)."

15. La Bonne Page operates through Facebook or through its own web address: www.librairie-labonnepage.com.

REFERENCES

Akomo-Zoghe, Cyriaque Simon-Pierre. 2010. *Parlons Fang: Culture et langue des Fang du Gabon et d'ailleurs*. Paris: L'Harmattan.

———. 2009. *L'art de conjuguer en fang*. Paris: L'Harmattan.

d'Almeida, Irène Assiba, ed. 2009. *A Rain of Words: A Bilingual Anthology of Women's Poetry in Francophone Africa*. Translated by Janis A. Mayes. Charlottesville: University of Virginia Press.

Endamne, Alice. 2008. *C'est demain qu'on s'fait la malle*. Saint-Maur-des-Fossés: Jets d'encre.

Essono, Fortunat Obiang. 2006. *Les registres de la modernité dans la littérature gabonaise: Maurice Okoumba Nkoghe, Laurent Owondo, et Justine Mintsa*. Vol. 2. Paris: L'Harmattan.

Gyasi, Kwaku. 2006. *The Francophone African Text: Translation and the Postcolonial Experience*. New York: Peter Lang.

Kandé, Sylvie. 2000. *Lagon, lagunes*. Paris: Gallimard.

Kuoh-Moukoury, Thérèse. 1969. *Rencontres essentielles*. Paris: Adamawa.

Liking, Werewere. 1996. *The Power of Um and a New Earth: African Ritual Theater*. Translated by Jeanne Dingome. San Francisco: International Scholars Press.

Mabanckou, Alain. 2006. "sos: pays africains cherchent désespérément des écrivains," April 17, 2006. http://www.congopage.com/sos-pays-africains -cherchent.

Mba Abessole, Paul. 2006. *Aux sources de la culture fang*. Paris: L'Harmattan.

Merey-Apinda, Edna. 2016. *Entre Nous*. Paris: La Doxa.

———. 2011. *Ce reflet dans le miroir*. Saint-Maur-des-Fossés: Jets d'encre.

———. 2004. *Les aventures d'Imya, petite fille du Gabon*. Paris: L'Harmattan.

Mintsa, Justine. 2010. *Larmes de cendre.* Béjaïa, Algeria: Éditions Tira.

———. 2000. *Histoire d'Awu.* Paris: Gallimard.

———. 1997. *Premières lectures.* Lomé: Haho.

———. 1994. *Un seul tournant: Makôsu.* Paris: La Pensée Universelle.

Mintsa, Justine Elo, and Grégory Ngbwa Mintsa. 2003. *Protocole du mariage coutumier au Gabon.* Libreville: Polypress.

Ngou, Honorine. 2007. *Mariage et Violence dans la société traditionnelle Fang au Gabon.* Paris: L'Harmattan.

Nguimbi, Arnold. 2012. "De la mort du maître a la mort symbolique de l'école: pour une pratique stylistique dans *Histoire d'Awu* de Justine Mintsa." In *La mort dans l'espace littéraire gabonais.* Edited by Clément Moupoumbou and Pierre Ndemby-Mamfoumby, 130–49. Libreville: Éditions Odette Maganga.

Ovono-Mendame, Jean-René. 2006. "Histoire d'Awu de Justine Mintsa: Entre soumission et révolte: les paradoxes d'un destin ambigu." *Africultures* (6 April 2006), http://www.africultures.com/php/index.php?nav=article&no=4368.

Rawiri, Angèle. 1980. *Elonga.* Paris: Silex.

Toman, Cheryl. 2016. *Women Writers of Gabon: Literature and Herstory.* Lanham MD: Lexington Books.

PART **ONE**

INTERLOCKING RINGS TOOK SHAPE, OBEDIENTLY LINING UP ONE after the other. With her tiny steel tool in hand, the focused miracle maker was unfazed as she toiled relentlessly, as if she had been desensitized to the beauty of her work. She seemed to have only one goal in mind: to accomplish her task for the day. Like a bee, she barely took any time at all to marvel over what she had created. She found nothing extraordinary in it. Her purpose in life was to create stitches, just as the bee's purpose was to produce honey. And the slender servant of the art was also there to continue making her small rings that connected one to the other, almost with pleasure, as if they were delighted to be linked, to belong to one other, to find meaning only in being together.

As for her thread, it never ceased to twist itself lasciviously under the unsympathetic yet steady stress of the iron instrument whose cold stiffness oddly contrasted with the inviting expression of the chain stitch.

Long, plump fingers with short fingernails guided the needle so skillfully that it seemed to move effortlessly. The thumb and index finger holding on to this tiny bit of iron with such reassurance and agility stitched the fabric that had been pierced with the help of the calculated efforts of a thimble-less middle finger. Suddenly all the fingers twitched, and from underneath the white fabric appeared a small spot of intense red. And almost immediately afterward, the wounded finger took off in search of comfort toward a gracious mouth that wasted no time in gently sucking and nibbling it; a mouth with thick lips whose harmonious contours were suddenly upset by this urgent need. At times the mouth formed two beautiful horizontal lines revealing a solid row of small, vertical rectangles the color of ivory; at other times the two lines converged toward their center to jut out like a suction cup. Two half circles just above these lips palpitated at the semi-salty taste of blood, while still higher, two normally bright celestial bodies were fading as the thick eyebrows that harbored them briefly knitted together. All of these waves produced themselves on a befreckled oblong face whose high forehead and pointed chin reminded one of a partridge egg.

Awudabiran' was the second wife of Obame Afane, the schoolteacher.

They say Obame's first wife died of a broken heart and that for six years she was unable to bear the fruit of a love consummated in intense moments of total ecstasy. But a man in Ebomane thought twice about purchasing land without the overwhelming evidence that it was indeed fertile; after six years of waiting, there was only one conclusion to be made.

When all hope was lost and he could no longer stand the pressure from the family, Obame Afame was forced to consider acquiring more fertile land, and he had to be absolutely certain that planting seeds there would yield an abundance of fruit, even without the ecstasy he so much enjoyed. Yet he feared that his beloved first wife would feel betrayed, even humiliated. She understood, however. She knew that this was the natural order of things and that, in fact, it was supposed to happen in this way. The fate of an arid plot of land, was it not to be abandoned for a more productive one? By marrying Obame Afame, however, she had become the mother of the entire village and one of the pillars of her husband's family. But in Ebomane, where the blessings of a household are measured in terms of its ability to reproduce, she knew that despite all her qualities, she did not have the *right* one. Arid lands do not choose to be arid, and yet it happens, much like fertile lands do not decide to be fertile. It comes down to luck. Some have it, others do not. You can perhaps push your luck, but it doesn't always work out. What else can you do besides resigning yourself to the facts?

One morning they found Obame's first wife dead in bed, even though she hadn't been sick. It just looked like she was sleeping peacefully. It was the same day Awudabiran' and Obame Afane's twins were born.

Awudabiran''s traditional marriage had taken place during her second pregnancy. Obame Afane had wanted to ensure that his land was indeed fertile before taking the plunge. Little Ondo Obame was proof of that—he was the twins' big brother.

Awu had been provided with a healthy dowry—and for good reason. She was the only woman in the entire region who held a degree! She was certified to teach elementary school and she was also a master seamstress! How could you not give a proper dowry to such a rare specimen? The family dispossessed of such an asset had to be consoled. Such a loss required good compensation, and what was offered was indeed on par. In exchange for their daughter, the family received a hefty sum and respectable quantities of *pagne*,[1] alcohol, and livestock. It was indeed understood that the purpose of this dowry was merely to concretize the implied agreement between the two families joined in marriage; the woman would be leaving to support her new family and to increase its size, which is why her in-laws in turn were supposed to express their gratitude by regularly aiding her parents. This was customary for any girl entering marriage. Only this time, in the case of Awudabiran', her diploma was a definite "plus," and it was indeed her in-laws who would reap the benefits of that, a fact that was terribly frustrating for her own parents. But after all, wasn't the husband a great schoolteacher himself, who was living in a beautiful terracotta brick home? There were not even ten such homes like that in the entire area. Soon Awu could very well be a grande dame in a big, sturdy house. This would be seen as a step up for the entire family, who had been used to seeing such brick houses only from afar; they themselves were living in homes made out of tree bark.

Obame Afane the schoolteacher had found fertile terrain in Awu-dabiran'. With the death of his first wife, he had lost a friend and partner. However, his second wife had now made him a full-fledged man. In Ebomane, anyone who did not ensure descendants was not a *man*. Nonetheless, now that his first wife was gone, Obame Afane could not help but feel a void that even the sight of his children and Awu could not fill.

Obame Afane had set his hopes on the lovely, young, and intelligent Awu. In his state of mind, he could not have known at the time that Awudabiran' was the last woman he should have chosen. Awu, in fact, expected so much from a man and from that very place in his heart that he wanted to forget about forever; he refused to betray his first wife by completely devoting himself to another woman. As for Awu, however, she had been saving herself for the man who would pick her among all of the possible choices in his garden. And for her, this man was Obame Afane.

Awu had always dreamed of sewing her life like a chain stitch: first tying a knot with children and marriage, then succeeding in every way through harmonious relationships in her married life as well as in her social and professional interactions. It is for this reason that throughout the duration of her studies, she remained like the closed bud of a flower. Once she acquired her professional standing, she wanted to blossom in the most complete fashion, basking in the warmth of love.

Even though her own father was polygamous, Awu was irritated to the very core of her being by the firm impression that she was still sharing her husband with her co-wife, even after her death. Of course, Awu had Obame all to herself every night, but she suspected that his mind was elsewhere while he was making love to her. She would have liked to have a man exclusively for her—body and soul, just for her. And to think that her own father had had two wives! And her mother had never complained of having her man all to herself just one out of two nights! But come to think of it, between Awu's mother, who had had her man all to herself every other night, and Awu, who had just half a man every night—who deserved the most sympathy? Strangely, when Awu would dream about her husband, she imagined him surrounded by a myriad of captivating smiles, the object of thousands of gazes and thousands of embraces. All the while he, with a distant look, was searching in vain to leave everything behind in order to join one woman in particular—but that woman was never Awu.

No, Obame Afane the schoolteacher didn't really know what type of terrain he had acquired. He had a general idea that the land was fertile and in great shape, which was a plus. But he didn't know that there was more to this land than just its fertility and good looks. He didn't know—and how could he have—that this land was in need of very special treatment.

With the coming of each dry season, Awudabiran' would fall hopelessly in love. Was it because of the way nature wore her dress of fire? In any case, this red-hot atmosphere used to set ablaze every single fiber of her being. Her lover was not anyone she could name. But in her mind, she knew exactly what features he had. If she had to sketch his image, she would be forced to make many of them, each one highlighting a major aspect of his appearance. It was not like he was an ensemble of disjointed parts, however. No, her lover was, in fact, a puzzle in which each piece mattered and held its independent meaning apart from the whole. As Awu pictured in her mind each one of these features in succession and up close, the rest would fade away into the shadows; it seemed to her that her lover could be metamorphosed just as many times, spontaneously generating just as many emotions and feelings in her heart and throughout her body.

Although Awu's husband was proud of her, he would never really look at her. For example, she would walk with much grace while balancing her sewing basket atop her head—she had a natural grace and was well aware of it. Yet Obame would only take a peek at her as she came toward him, and all the while she was yearning for him to be captivated by her and to show this through an honest, deliberate, and, of course, admiring look. So in her dreams her lover became those Eyes, eyes whose glance was somewhere between persuasive and domineering, eyes that were all over her, staring at her, exploring her, then contemplating her. Just the thought of this would leave her feeling as light as air, radiant, overwhelmed.

As for Obame Afane, he made it a source of honor to be a good father and a responsible husband.

Sometimes, when Obame had no papers to grade in the evening, he would go outside to tell stories. On such occasions, it was inevitably his brother Nguema Afane's job to build a large, wood-burning fire in the courtyard. For his trouble, the villagers always rewarded Nguema with at least two bottles of sugar cane wine and some *malamba*,[2] which gave him the energy necessary to fan the fire until his brother finished. It didn't matter which hill the children came from; they were all permanently enchanted by those stories. At home, Obame also meticulously nurtured the development of his own children.

At other times and for no specific reason, he would surprise Awu with spools of multicolored thread. Or he would bring her back some brightly colored scraps of poplin or percale. Or better still, he would entrust her with a few kilos of meat along with one or two superb pagnes for her to give to her parents.

On some evenings he would arrive earlier than expected, handing over a package to his children and declaring:

"Fresh gazelle! Go give it to your mother. We'll eat it tonight!"

The children would present their mother with the meat, and their father would rush to cut it up for her.

After several years of marriage, however, Awu's husband had never taken her into his arms the way she would have liked—not even once. Whenever she thought about such an embrace, Arms and Hands would appear in her head—sturdy arms and large hands perfect for holding her by the waist, her slim waist that villagers liked to criticize. A good mother, they used to say, was supposed to be pleasantly plump; it was a sign of fertility, good health, and well-being. Although her husband never complained, Awu knew very well that because of her waist, still slim even after several pregnancies, she was not considered by the village to be a canon of beauty. Yet she would have sacrificed everything to stay so slender. She was determined to do so more than anything else, for it was her secret hope that one day her husband would deliver her from her obsession; he would simply hold her by the waist and squeeze her tightly, so tight that it would take her breath away. And that would be it; she would be satisfied. This wish was so simple that she felt it almost childish. Until now, however, she had never once in her life seen a man embrace a woman in the way she was dreaming about. She did not even know if such a thing were possible. But her body silently, yet passionately, yearned for it. When she would gather up pieces of material to stitch together, pulling on the thread to enclose the fabric inside a ringlet, this bit of cloth so powerfully embraced would remind her of the strength of those Arms around her waist. This feeling was so intense that at times, it would leave her breathless to the point where she almost passed out, sometimes while even out in public.

When the lover in her head would transform himself into the Voice—a sweet, warm, reassuring, and convincing voice—no other sound was capable of reaching Awu's ears. Sometimes upon hearing this voice, Awu would respond softly, and the sound of her own words would make her jump and frighten the Voice, who then sought to move away from this partner who had violated the boundaries of the dream.

Awu didn't care if it was good or bad to let herself be bombarded by all these images and sensations. She was quite simply happy to have a secret garden and congratulated herself for hiding these desires so perfectly well.

Awu was convinced that her true wedding day would be the actual day this embrace would finally become a reality. She and her husband would both be liberated; she from an obsession, he from a specter.

OBAME AFANE WAS RELIEVED TO HEAR THE ROOSTER CROW. HE had lost nothing in the transition from night to day. The moans and groans of nocturnal beasts had progressively been replaced by the rhythms and greetings of diurnal animals of the nearby forest; in the village, gossip and grumbling announced the dawn. Daylight was determined to force its way into the bedroom in the form of vertical batons of light that made all the more noticeable the badly fitting window frames—constant reminders of how poor the workmanship really was. If those frames could talk, they would surely complain to the carpenter, letting him know how he had betrayed his craft, as if they were sure that the home's two occupants would have agreed with them. It wasn't such a misguided idea, judging by the looks of the rest of the room and its contents.

The best view of the bedroom was from the entryway, which looked directly onto the living room. From the vantage point of the outswinging entry door, the bedroom initially revealed a great deal of intimacy. A large bed made of bully-tree wood stood against the back wall and graced the center of the room. The bed had been skillfully smoothed out and assembled piece by piece using age-old craftsmanship; every detail had been done by hand. A short, sturdy stool flanked each side of the bed. In front of one stool sat an outdated, square-shaped crib with rungs of disproportionate size. In the corner a huge armoire topped with two imposing tin trunks seemed to watch over everything. With legs shamelessly rivaling pillars more typically found on a house, a solid wood table was planted against the back wall next to the other stool. Across from the table sat a sad piece of furniture suffering its own identity crisis—it was neither a bench nor a chair, but could pass for either one. Nearby, a practically empty bookcase stood with its sturdy, frustrated shelves resigned to the fact that their strength was of no use. On each side of the only door to the room, enamel bowls and rattan baskets lined the wall.

Daylight made its official entrance into the room through one of two openings: either the one situated above the crib, which gave the morning light the allure of an angel's glow, or the other in front of the solid wood table. With the rising sun, each item in the room exited from the night to reveal itself in daylight.

All the gleaming woodwork was dark brown. The two tin trunks were cassava-leaf green. The two stools were covered with identical mats, both finely embroidered and abundant in color. On the table were two piles of notebooks, one of open notebooks stacked one on top of the other alongside a second pile of closed ones. A smoky glass kerosene lamp sat in the middle of the table and just next to that, a feather pen was soaking in its red inkwell. A wooden ruler was standing on alert alongside the pile of closed notebooks. The bowls contained dirty laundry and the baskets, clean clothes. Everything was neatly organized except for the bed and the crib, which their occupants had deserted shortly after daylight invaded.

"You didn't sleep at all last night," Awu said as she followed her husband along the little path, protected by mahogany trees and lined with tall bushes, which led to the river bank.

No matter what Awu said to him, Obame just sighed.

"Everything will be back to normal soon," she went on. "Stop being so negative. After all, a child is a blessing, isn't it?"

"But she's so young, Awu. She's only twelve. And her pregnancy is almost full term. And she's been expelled from school. It's over for her. It's finished for this child, finished! Do you understand? And here I am beating myself, telling everyone else's children what to do, alerting their parents about this very thing. Why did this have to happen to the daughter of my own sister? She put all her hope in her daughter. We put all our hope in her! And all this just as I am about to retire! It's like all those years of preaching morality and teaching countless lessons were for nothing!"

With these words, Obame had stopped to turn toward his wife who, likewise, could do nothing but sigh after each word. They remained like this for a few seconds, face to face, contemplative, motionless.

At that moment Obame Afane the schoolteacher was wearing the very same expression that had won over Awu some years ago, when he had come to supervise final exams at the school to which she had just been assigned. She was eighteen years old at the time. It was her first year in the profession, and she was intimidated by her older and more experienced colleagues such as Obame Afane, even though he himself was only in his thirties at the time. Since the first impression he had created for her was one of toughness, Awu was always taken aback when he addressed her in a friendly, almost warm tone. She had imagined him to be disapproving and critical. What a look he had on his face when he realized during that same exam period that Mengara, one of his best students, was absent! He had asked one or two of Mengara's classmates if they had seen him. But neither one had. So around noon, while the other teachers were heading toward the cafeteria for lunch, Obame the schoolteacher took it upon himself to go on foot to Nkoaman—a tiny, remote village two kilometers away from the school—to find out why his student was absent. During lunch, word of this spread very quickly among the teachers. Awu was more than impressed. She was bursting with admiration. Obame the schoolteacher even came back in time for the afternoon exam. He told those who were interested that Mengara—who was already motherless—had just lost his grandmother the night before the exam. His face at that moment expressed so much frustration and powerlessness that it touched Awu at the very core of her being: Obame the schoolteacher was the universal father.

He had that exact same impression talking about his niece's problem that morning. All of a sudden, the child that Awu was carrying on her back started crying as if to jumpstart her parents back in motion; they resumed walking shortly thereafter. Arriving at the water's edge, they strolled along the bank until they reached a clearing surrounded by interwoven shrubbery. There, with her right hand, Awu untied from her chest the two knots of her pagne designed to hold the baby on her back, while with her left hand she supported the baby's little behind as she wedged its tiny hands under her own armpits. Once the two pieces of the pagne were free, she caught the tiny left hand with her right one and pulled onto her chest the pint-sized person who continued to whine. The little girl was about one year old. To calm her down, Awu offered the baby her breast for about ten minutes while sitting on her pagne spread out on the ground, her back propped against a tree trunk positioned right in the middle of where they were. From that spot, she could once again admire her husband in peace. He had undressed and dove into the river screaming and thrashing about to get warm; the water was so cold in the morning! Soon, he emerged onto the bank and chose the softest, best-shaped lump of clay. He lathered his entire body. Then he began to scrub himself energetically. He rinsed off and came back once more to soap up, this time using a bar of French soap that he again lathered onto his body. He had wide shoulders and strong arms, with muscles like instruments playing the rhythms of all the massaging and lathering. He left some soap for his wife and kids. When he had finished, he again went toward the river and surrendered his body to the whims of the water. Sometimes he swam on his side, then turned over on his stomach, executing an entertaining butterfly stroke, rhythmically disappearing and reappearing; other times he was lying on his back facing the sun, swimming the backstroke along with the current. He expressed himself with such freedom and independence that Awu was almost jealous of that river. To finish up, he did enormous breaststrokes toward the shore. And Awu thought to herself: "He's coming back to me."

For decades he had been devoting himself to this ritual, on this same rock. He was born a few meters from here, precisely on the spot where his wife was breastfeeding her child. That was almost fifty years ago now.

That was the year in which Ebomane had just gotten its own public school; prior to that, the rather large village only had an evangelical school, a source of both pride and contempt. But now a real school in the village! The kids no longer had to trek twenty kilometers every single day just to get an education! And what's more, at the new school at least, no one was going to denigrate the religion of the Ancestors like they did at the missionary school!

Obame Afane's father, Afane Obame, was a high priest of *Melan*[3] worship. This ritual worship was celebrated every Saturday evening until dawn. You could hear the *tam-tams*[4] resound from miles around.

The evangelical mission was located on the other end of the village; it was a bit set back on the top of a small hill. Afane Obame's father, Obame Evouna, himself a high priest, had stood by and watched the mission being built on the other end of his village. He hadn't fought against it because it had no impact on what he did on his own hill. In his view, it posed no threat to the religion of the Ancestors. And that was the most important thing.

The village was, in fact, located between two hills. At the top of one hill stood a little church whose doors and windows were perpetually left open, and a slender cross was displayed above. And the other hill was capped with gigantic trees whose trunks were flanked by bushes and shrubs.

Those indeed were the two temples of Ebomane—the Cross-Topped Hill and the Wood-Girded Hill.

The inauguration of the new school took place the first day of the academic year. And it was just at that moment when the whole village was arriving for the event that Oyane, Obame Afane's mother, began to experience abdominal pain. At first she thought she needed to relieve herself. But by the time she got behind the main kitchen to the little shed that housed the septic tank, she realized that her bladder wasn't full, but she crouched down anyway. Nothing came out. After a difficult time getting back up, she was moving along at a snail's pace toward the little doorway when she felt an urgent need to defecate. She twisted and turned and practically limped back so she could crouch down over the hole once more. Two, five, ten minutes went by. Nothing. Fifteen minutes. Still nothing. In order to lift herself up again, she had to get up on all fours and move forward in that position until she could at least reach the door to hold on and catch herself at times when the pain was too intense. She had felt a stubborn, general, and irregular pain that was quickly growing in intensity and becoming excruciating. When the pain seemed to subside a bit, she seized the moment to head over, like a wounded elephant, toward the nearby kitchen that her mother-in-law was starting to close up.

"God in heaven!" her mother-in-law exclaimed at the sight of Oyane, unlocking the door at once. "There's no time to spare! Start walking toward the river. I'll take what we need and meet you there."

She arrived a few minutes later to find out that Oyane hadn't even arrived there yet since she was forced to stop along the way to sit on the ground when the pain was too much for her; she would pick up her slow, uncomfortable, and laborious pace only when the pain subsided a bit. When Oyane finally reached the riverbank, her mother-in-law rushed up to her, guiding her to a tiny clearing a few steps away, a clearing carpeted in the center by three big, beautiful, banana-tree leaves. Oyane lay down on them. A moment later the mountains echoed triumphantly the gut-wrenching cry of this birth, replaced soon thereafter by a little scream whose vigor and vitality rivaled those of the rhythms and greetings of diurnal animals. Obame Afane had arrived.

While the baby was laying close to his mother on the banana-tree leaf, the Nourishing Mass that had fed him for nine months, its mission accomplished, began liberating itself from its point of attachment, painfully, regretfully, but victoriously. Finally the end of the delivery was near. The mass of tissue, soft and still throbbing, showed itself at the Door of Life and was soon expelled. All red in the face, Oyane moaned, sad and happy at the same time, waiting for the next part. It wouldn't take long: In one quick move, Oyane's mother-in-law wrapped the mass in two large, glossy banana-tree leaves. Then she picked up the sharp, little, blood-stained machete that had separated Obame Afane from his mother. With an agile step, she traveled back up the path that led to the village, stopped halfway, and went off-trail. Soon she arrived at the foot of a clump of banana trees, and with her machete she furiously began to dig a hole in the soft, fertile ground. When the hole was deep enough to fit three plantains end to end, she stopped digging, set her machete off to the side, and opened up the bundle she had transported. The Mass of Life saw the light of day one last time before taking up residence in its new womb: that of the earth—this same earth that it would also rejuvenate. If the Nourishing Mass had the power to see, it would have observed, from the bottom of its hole, a face leaning over it, with closed eyes and lips praying over it; it would have also noticed the two hands kneading a little lump of earth drenched with spit to make a sort of mud, which those same hands then rubbed onto the face. And if this Mass of Life had indeed the power to hear, it would have learned by way of Obame Afane's grandmother's prayer that it was being given a new mission—to fertilize and impregnate the earth, to itself produce in order to sustain the life of men and women who were themselves called upon to perpetuate the lineage. By slathering her face with this mud, this grandmother had sealed a pact with the earth and thus they shared a common mission—to perpetuate life. A moment later, the Mass of Life assumed its new role in communion with the earth as the soil closed in on it.

"He shall be named Sikolo. He was born at the same time as the village school," whispered the grandmother as she made her way back.

Grandmother had told Obame Afane the story of his birth dozens of times, always omitting the part about the placenta. A week after his circumcision, however, his grandmother took him to the exact spot where he was born. He was six years old at the time. Although he had started to heal from his circumcision, he was still wearing large *boubous*.[5] There, at his birthplace, his grandmother rolled out before him an old pagne that enveloped a hard object. A small machete was slowly revealed. His grandmother said to him:

"Look at this machete. It's small but very sharp. It can easily be concealed. You couldn't even tell that I had been carrying it in the pocket of my *kaba*,[6] could you? To see the light of day, you came out of the Door of Life head first. That means that you will become a righteous man. That's why I had used this blade as straight and radiant as a ray of sun. It has never been used since. Your younger brother, Nguema Afane, was born exposing his bottom to the Door of Life: that was a bad sign. That's why I didn't use a machete to separate Nguema Afane from his mother, who took her last breath as he took his first, but rather I chose *ôkenguen be kône*[7]—a blade made from plants as sharp as a razor. That's what's done in these kinds of cases. Here, take this machete. It's yours. It separated you from your mother at birth. It binds you to your ancestors, yet separates them from you at the same time. Keep it preciously. It's a keepsake. It's as simple as that."

So Obame Afane grew up with this object always tucked away in a secret place known only to him. And each time he came to swim, a few steps away from the place where he had been born, it was like a rebirth for him.

Obame came out of the water to grab his towel. He had left it behind on the tree trunk, there where his wife was sitting. He said to her:

"It's your turn. Leave the child with me."

Awu set the little girl down onto the pagne spread out on the ground, and in one swift move she undid her pagne, which was wrapped around her. The contact with the cold water caused Awu to arch her back. She eventually plunged into the water that came up to her shoulders and soon began bobbing up and down and spinning around.

For Sikolo Obame Afane, who was supposed to preside over a family meeting a few hours later, this swim was not exactly routine.

THAT SAME SATURDAY, AS THE SUN ROSE PROGRESSIVELY TOWARD high noon, the extended family invaded Sikolo Obame Afane's house little by little.

Young people and neighbors alike were observing from the outside veranda, sitting on the ground, or pressed up against the window pane.

In the large salon that served as the meeting room, the Elders sat and formed a circle, closing in on the object of their attention: Ada.

Ada's grandfather had four children: a daughter, Ntsame Afane, who had gone to live in the city; a son, Nguema Afane, who had two wives and nineteen children; another son, Sikolo Obame Afane; and another daughter, Okut Afane, who was Ada's mother. Once all of the members of the Family Council had gathered, Ada's grandfather began to speak, and in a hoarse yet resounding voice, he said:

"Obame, we have all come down from the mountain to gather at your house. Of course, as an elder, I am the one who is supposed to host you at my home. But as the little one is not well and her presence at this meeting is necessary, I preferred to come down instead."

After these words, there was a pause so long that you could have heard a fly buzzing about. Then grandfather spoke again:

"Your younger sister, Akut Afane, is in mourning. Do you realize this?"

"Yes, Father, I know," answered Obame Afane.

Then, addressing the other family members present, the grandfather asked in a booming voice:

"All of you who are gathered here, do you know that my daughter Akut Afane is in mourning?"

"Yes, we know," answered the elders in unison.

"Aren't all of us gathered here from the same bloodline? All branches of the same tree?"

"That's exactly right," the chorus rang out again.

"So, if all of this is indeed true, aren't you curious as to why it is only Akut Afane in mourning? How can one broken branch fundamentally change the tree? Last night, at the hour the owls were screeching, my daughter came to announce to me that she had lost her daughter. Do you hear me? Ada Ondo, here in front of me, sitting between her Uncle Obame Afane and her Aunt Awudabiran', is apparently no longer alive. Let Obame Afane explain to us what has happened to his sister and her daughter. I'm done talking."

With these very words, all eyes turned first toward Ada before converging on Obame Afane. As much as her extra weight would allow, Ada huddled between Awu and her uncle, at whose house she had shown up last night in a sorry state. She had gotten pregnant while away at school, just before summer break. When Ada had returned to the village, her mother didn't notice a thing as the girl had hid her condition very well. Ada was in *cinquième*, boarding at a provincial *collège*[8] about twenty miles away from Ebomane. The pregnancy evolved considerably in the course of the school year to the point where hiding it became practically impossible; consequently, her secret no longer was a secret, and the school's administrators decided to expel her. Her mother was summoned to pick her up. Ada was practically full term. In the bus on the way back, no words were exchanged between mother and daughter. It was only upon arriving in Ebomane, as they were getting off the bus, that her mother had blurted out to her daughter matter-of-factly: "You are not to set foot in my house. In my mind, you are dead." In hearing these words, Ada lowered her head and sat down on her tiny suitcase, watching her mother distance herself from her as the bus drove off in the opposite direction. The somber veil of nightfall began to enshroud the large village. Ada was somewhat relieved by the timing of this as she didn't want to be recognized. A moment later she managed to get back on her feet and, with her suitcase atop her head, she walked into the night toward her Uncle Obame Afane's house.

As grandfather had allowed him to speak, Obame Afane got up, looking very serious; his eyes swept across everyone in the room. He then glared at his sister Akut who was directly in front of him, sitting on the floor between two chairs occupied by Elders. With her disheveled hair and her pagne attached haphazardly just above her breasts, she offered up an image that was angry as well as resentful. Then, turning toward his father, Obame Afane said:

"When my daughter Ada arrived at my house yesterday at nightfall, I could tell right away that a terrible misfortune had befallen this family. And why? Akut isn't married and doesn't have a job. She turned her back on school very early on. And then she had never wanted to marry. My sister always preferred the easy route. School was too hard and marriage too confining. Years went by, and Akut saw that her former classmates were doing well socially and professionally. She began to regret her choices bitterly. This has to be said here today. It's something everyone knows. And it's the truth. And everyone knows what I think about this. She never wanted to follow my example—that of her older brother—as she figured that a woman didn't need to struggle in life in order to succeed. After coming to her senses, Akut wanted to make up for lost time and redeem herself by becoming the woman she should have or could have always been: an educated woman, financially independent, and happily married. I know that my sister completely forgot about her past and was living only for the day when this dream would become reality. Do you hear me?"

"We hear you," answered the crowd in unison.

"But do you understand what I'm saying to you?"

"Speak, Obame Afane, your words are as clear as the waters of Assok,[9] retorted one of the Elders.

"I'm indeed saying that Akut no longer lives for herself but only for and through her daughter and everything she represents. As you all know, the only path to true success in today's world is through education and good judgment. But unfortunately, no other woman in this family has ever had such ambition. Ada is the first in whom we all truly believed. She became everyone's hope for the future. And personally, she was my own pride and joy. Now look. Look at her. In the condition that she's in, she can forget about school and a good life. Ada's success was her mother's reason for living. Now do you understand, Father, why your daughter is in mourning?"

Ada, her head lowered, did not stop sobbing throughout Obame Afane's entire speech. From time to time she blew her nose loudly using the kaba Awu had given her the night before in a discreet effort to console her. A heavy silence hung over the room before the grandfather responded:

"My son, you have spoken. I don't know if what you said is right. I don't know if what you said is wrong. As for me, I'm from the old school. You, you are a man of today. We don't see things in the same way. This explains why I cannot grasp the nature of the misfortune that befalls you. Fertile land has always been a blessing in Ebomane. But I am just realizing that today it can be considered a curse. Your first wife—didn't she die of a broken heart because of her infertility? Everyone here knows how much you loved her, but a real woman knows this is not enough. Women were meant to have children. It is a vital need not only for her, but above all, it is also a duty greater than no other. Nothing else really matters. If you young people are alarmed because a woman has accomplished this duty just a little earlier than expected and consider that the life she carries within her is symbolic of death, I must admit to you that your new way of seeing things is beyond my comprehension. Next you'll be telling me that a dead leaf can stand up to the wind, or that a child can give birth to his mother. The man you see before you, it is I who am truly out of touch with reality. Out of touch! That being said, I, Afane Obame, am leaving. Where are the twins? Bring me back to the mountain!"

Nguema Afane's twins, two fifteen-year-old, good-looking guys, rushed up to their grandfather and each took an arm. Just when the grandfather was about to get up, Awu's father, who had arrived two days earlier to bring his son-in-law's family some goods from his hunting trip and who, quite logically, attended the elders' meeting as a member of the extended family, asked Afane Obame to remain seated. All the young people in Ebomane knew Awu's father. They admired him very much because he was a major supporter of their soccer team. All the young people were proud of him because he was a grandfather who was "cool." "Serious, but cool," they insisted.

As in-laws are considered sacred, Afane Obame didn't have a choice in the matter. Furthermore, it was the duty of the spouses' elders, known as *Mbebeñ*, to maintain particularly courteous relationships with one another. So Afane Obame settled back into his seat once again, ready to listen to his peer, his *Mui*.

"*Mui Mbebeñ*," began Awu's father, "the whole family is gathered here to resolve a problem that I consider very serious. Indeed, it involves the lives of our children. The problem has been put here before us. The children have let their thoughts be known. And you as well have let your thoughts be known. Everyone has argued his point of view. And these two points of view are diametrically opposed. Am I wrong?"

"You speak the truth, oh *Mui Mbebeñ*."

"So we cannot part ways like this. True, I am an outsider. But because of the ties that bind us, your problems are mine. And vice versa. So it's with just cause that I am going to intervene in this affair. Are you all ears?"

"All ears, oh *Mui*."

"What is done is done. The little one is pregnant and she's been expelled from school. Elders 1, Youth 0. That's the score, isn't it?"

"That's exactly right," the crowd agreed.

"Obame Afane!" he continued, "You who teach at the white school, tell me just one thing. The banana tree has only one chance in its existence to offer up the best that it can. Is this the same for a student attending the white school? I'm listening."

"*Minkî*, father-in-law," said Obame Afane, "you're getting ahead of me. Your question brings up a very important point that I had intended to address after presenting the current situation. Our daughter has disappointed us, that's true. She has dishonored some among us. This is also true. But the question that we all should be asking ourselves right now is if it is utterly impossible for her to return to school. *Minkî*, in answer to your question, I am speaking to everyone gathered here to solemnly proclaim that our daughter Ada is not beyond redemption. If her delivery goes well, she still has the possibility of returning to school and making up the time lost . . . provided that she has the will to do so, provided that this is what she really wants."

"*Nnom ngon*, son-in-law, the words you have just spoken sound as sweet as honey. You have just doused the fires of our hot heads with cool water. *Nnom ngon*, our hearts are beating at a normal pace once again. Dear friends, this isn't a game. Or if it is, the score is tied. Am I lying about this?"

"We don't even know what you mean by that word," the crowd snapped back.

"My job here is done," said Awu's father, readjusting his large *boubou* before settling into his armchair to comfortably follow along with the turn of events to come.

Afane Obame, who knew perfectly well that it would come down to his decision alone, cleared his throat to force silence upon the crowd and said:

"*Mui Mbebeñ*, I believe everything has been said. I have not much more to add, and it's my pleasure to confirm that there is no problem here. No problem at all. Akut, bring your daughter home. Be considerate of her and take care of her needs. Her condition is sacred. Sacred, I tell you."

Little by little, people began to disperse. Soon, only the residents of the house and Akut remained. She had waited for everyone to leave before lashing out at her brother:

"Obame, my position hasn't changed. As far as I'm concerned, Ada no longer exists. I want nothing to do with her or with the child she is carrying. You say that she is not beyond redemption. So in that case, you can rehabilitate her yourself!"

On this note, she took off without waiting for a reaction. Ada collapsed, and Awu began to console her the best that she could. She had been Ada's moral support for the entire duration of the gathering. As she was coddling the sobbing Ada, Awu had even thought she had detected a glimmer of relief mixed with gratefulness behind Akut's livid look. But now Awu was convinced that Akut was abandoning her daughter simply because she didn't want to take care of her, and especially not in her current condition. Thus, neither Obame nor Awu attempted to go after Akut to reason with her; they feared that in doing so, Ada would feel that she was unwanted in their home as well.

ADA LIVED WITH THE COUPLE WITHOUT INCIDENT. SHE WAS quiet and obedient. Following her aunt's recommendation, she sucked on slices of salted lemon when she suffered from morning sickness. She submitted ungrudgingly to the demands of prenatal care: swallowing each night a half-liter of sticky, unsalted snail bouillon thought to shorten labor, gulping down salt-free okra pods for a healthier amniotic fluid, chewing on smoked eel's tail to prevent the baby's buttocks from passing through the birth canal first, refraining from eating porcupine, of which she was particularly fond, so that the baby wouldn't be born with a cleft lip—and these were just some of the many sacrifices and hardships. Awu subjected Ada to the same treatment from which she herself had benefited while pregnant.

There was no doubt that Ada's stay in Obame Afane's house was responsible for bringing together two people who had long remained strangers, even after years of living in the same house. Those two people were Ntsame Afane, the eldest sister of Obame Afane, and Awu.

Ntsame had lived in the city at one time. She spent time with whites, then later with black revolutionaries who were fighting for independence. In Ebomane they used to say that city life had changed her because when she finally returned, she was no longer considered a good woman. Not only had she never wanted children, but she willingly chose the single life and never even entertained the thought of one day getting married. And furthermore she spent too much time thinking and just as much time talking—like a know-it-all. And moreover, she knew how to stand up to men. Not a good thing. For a woman, that wasn't a good thing at all. But she could care less about what the village thought of her. The only reason she had come back was to forget about a lover that had been gunned down and killed.

Since Ada's arrival at Awu's, Ntsame stopped by practically every evening to enquire about her niece's health. At such times she would very often ask her sister-in-law Awu about her work. And she herself would talk about her tumultuous past. She would speak passionately about the ideologies of the political figures whom she had met and unabashedly confessed how tender certain lovers among them had been for her. After one week of such visits, the two women had made up for all those years of indifference they had maintained in the past. They had forged themselves a sincere friendship accompanied by a hint of complicity and mutual admiration.

Quite often Ada's cousins—the children of Nguema Afane, Obame Afane's younger brother—also came to visit. They always conveniently arrived at lunchtime, and one didn't exactly have to beg them to partake. After all, wasn't their uncle's house their house too? Sometimes their stay would run on into the evening meal. On such occasions Ntsame would reserve for them a frosty greeting upon her arrival. She thought they were lazy and also irresponsible, just like their father, whose house she hardly ever set foot in. Because Ntsame's attitude toward her nephews changed the mood in the house considerably, the boys were inclined to slip away, asking their cousin to accompany them part of the way home. Ntsame took advantage of the situation to vent her disapproval:

"Here are the very people in the family who make me sick! A guy like that, without a permanent job, who attaches himself to two women and who contents himself with producing at least one brat per year! Ever since cocoa sales have dropped off, he survives by picking up women, or through kickbacks and deceit, whereas we have suggested to him 1,001 times how he can diversify his crop production by planting bananas, for example, that require hardly any initial capital and almost no upkeep. Opportunities abound with all the missionaries and civil servants that regularly come to shop at the Ebomane market every Thursday. But no . . . the man prefers to spend his time whining about his fate and coercing his family to help him. With these two hearty sons, he could have continued to thrive. When his brother's business began to decline, Obame Afane decided to take his two oldest nephews under his wing. He took them in so that they could continue their studies without any worries. But by the end of the year, he sent them back to their parents. He could no longer stand their behavior—the impoliteness, the showing off, the lying, the laziness, and the nastiness. Any remark made by Obame's first wife had set them off and sent them running to their parents with unwarranted complaints punctuated unfortunately with a remark about Bella's infertility—they were supposedly mistreated because they are the sons of a farmer. They were being looked after by an infertile woman who didn't hesitate to ask them to do the dishes after the meal because she was worn out from cooking; they had to wash their own clothes even though she had plenty of time to do her husband's laundry, or they had to sweep the house early in the morning because she didn't have enough time after returning from the market, etc. etc.

Now Awu, I swear to you, after six years of marriage, no one ever considered this poor woman as just the daughter-in-law or the sister-in-law. *M'bôm* or *M'mieñ*. She was everyone's daughter, everyone's sister, everyone's mother. Through marriage she had become one of the pillars of this family. However, no matter what she did, nothing could compensate for her handicap. But she knew this was how things were. She understood that. She accepted it. She was forgiving. However, her husband didn't see things the same way. He revolted and rebelled against all this injustice, especially when learning that people in the village held her 'disability' against her and figured that she owed it to her in-laws to wait on them hand and foot. This calabash of patience that was Obame Afane boiled over one night when his nephews had the audacity to enter her bedroom and drop off their dirty laundry. Their aunt did not touch it. She preferred to let her husband find it first.

'What is this all about?' asked Obame as he left his bedroom displaying the bag that filled the tiny living room with a strong odor of sweat. His wife was setting the table and pretended not to hear a thing. His two nephews, who were in the middle of a game of *songo*,[10] suddenly stopped what they were doing. The oldest one glanced up and, looking his uncle straight in the eye, said:

'Summer break starts tomorrow and so we want to go home right after our last class.'

'Well, thanks for taking the time to tell me. But I would still like to know what this bag is doing on my bed. To whom does it belong? Bella, are you listening to me?'

'Obame, I too, like you, only just discovered it a few moments ago. I don't know who put it there.'

'So who is responsible for putting this sack on my bed?' exploded Obame Afane.

'We did,' said the oldest nephew. 'Rather, I did,' he specified. 'We wanted our laundry to be ready before we leave.'

After this response, Obame took a seat in the living room, placed the bag on the floor next to his armchair, and remained silent for a long while, staring at each one of his nephews in turn and shaking his head. Finally he said:

'You wanted your laundry to be done before you leave, is that right? And so it will be, don't worry. Isn't that right, Bella? I guess this is for you then,' said Obame, holding out the stinking bundle of clothes to his wife.

"And do you know what, Awu?" Ntsame continued. "Later, Obame confided in me that he had forced his wife to endure all those hardships so that she could find favor with the gods and become fertile. The laundry was duly washed, starched, and pressed. Then Obame left to take his nephews back to their father. For good. But, alas! Awu, the years went by, and Bella still wasn't able to bear the fruits of their love. When all hope was lost, and Obame was under pressure from all sides—both from his own family and from Bella—he had to seriously consider acquiring more fertile terrain, and he had to already be certain he could sow there, all pleasure aside, fruits that would proliferate in abundance. Forgive me, will you, Awu? I am not saying that my brother loves you less, but I am just telling you what happened. And when his wife died, he was terribly hard on himself and he still is today. So you can understand why I don't have a place in my heart for those two thankless kids. They ruthlessly and needlessly made my poor sister-in-law suffer. And all those loud mouths in the village went along with it and didn't say a word. It's sickening, yes. I really think those kids will find themselves in hot water one day. What goes around, comes around."

Just as Ntsame had said these words, Ada came back to sit next to her Aunt Awu. She loved and respected her. These were the only two women Ada felt she could trust. She knew that Aunt Ntsame wasn't crazy about her situation, but she never uttered a single harsh word toward her either. Ntsame's presence was even somewhat reassuring. At some point in a woman's life, she needs to feel close to someone on her mother's side of the family. Ntsame's daily visits gave Ada a sense of security now that her own mother had abandoned her in this condition. She felt a sort of reassurance that even all of Awu's care and tenderness couldn't provide, even though Ada was very grateful for it. Some unknown feeling inside made her long to get close to a woman who shared the same blood.

"Did you go far?" Awu asked her.

"No," answered Ada staring at the floor. "I stopped to sit under the giant *atangatier*[11] with the blue dates, and we talked a bit before going our separate ways."

"They have no business coming around here trying to influence you, you got that? Do you understand? There are already enough problems as it is."

Ada had appreciated her aunt using precisely the words "there are problems." The formidable Aunt Nstame, who feared no one, still had the sensitivity to not terrorize her—a little girl in the wrong— with a more traumatic "you have problems" instead. Ada felt so good in the presence of these two women who loved her that she all of a sudden came out and said:

"I'm sorry."

She paused for a bit. Then she continued:

"I've wanted to ask for forgiveness for a long time. But I'm not sure whom to ask for it or how. Forgive me, but I'm not a bad girl at all. I've never insulted anyone and I never wanted to hurt anybody. Just a bit ago, Aunt Ntsame told me not to allow my cousins to be a bad influence on me. But how could I let that happen, knowing that I don't approve of their behavior? When they behaved badly with Aunt Bella I was still very young, but I was old enough to know that what they were doing was very wrong. And I still believe so. So please . . . I made a mistake getting pregnant, it's true, but please, please . . . don't take me for a bad girl. I'm not!"

Ada began sobbing bitterly, but neither of the two women made an effort to console her. A moment later, she blew her nose loudly using the tail of her dress, wiped her cheeks with the backside of her hand, and with her eyes still lowered, she let out a big sigh.

PART **TWO**

OBAME AFANE HAD BEEN INFORMED BY RADIO THAT HE WAS indeed officially retired. One month later he decided to travel to the capital to put his pension file in order. Outside of the capital there was no office anywhere else in the country that took care of such matters.

Construction on Obame Afane the schoolteacher's new house, located not far from his childhood home was, in fact, not quite finished by the time he had to vacate the residence that had been provided to him as part of his terms of employment. Still awaiting permanent doors and windows, his new house was temporarily equipped with panels made of tree bark. The carpenter, Mezui Mba, had the doors and windows all ready to go—they just needed to be paid for. But what mattered most to Awudabiran' was to have a large wooden table in her living room where she could display her various fashionable creations. After so much sewing for others, she wanted to treat herself for once and feast her eyes on enchanting views and surroundings. So she insisted that everything be ready by the following dry season so that she could take advantage of the vacation period to move into the house for good.

What excitement there was in the village the night before Obame's departure for the capital!

Pastor Gambier and a few missionaries had come by very early in the morning to wish Obame a good trip and a productive stay. Shortly before he left they prayed for him and his family.

A council of the most revered elders gathered shortly thereafter to bestow bits of wisdom upon Obame and to give him their blessing.

Komandé, the former chief of police who had himself retired three years ago, advised Obame about what documents he needed to produce and the offices he had to contact. He did point out, however, that his own file had still not gone through all the proper channels and he didn't understand why; he was hoping that the next cocoa crop would give him enough cash so that he could pay for his return to the capital to find out. He didn't know anybody there who could take care of his file for him.

Komandé described the capital to him as a place where he should be on alert for all kinds of traps: roads, thieves, alcohol, women.

Those who had never been to the capital just simply wished him good luck.

The women were present but kept silent except for Ntsame, who in the most aggressive way she knew how made sure she got in a last word:

"Just leave already. Nothing is going to happen to you. Everything will be fine. Our gods and our ancestors are with you. For over thirty years now, you've been tearing yourself out of your wife's arms to take a dive in the river at the crack of dawn before going to work—with eyes barely open and legs that could hardly carry you there. For thirty years, chalk dust has filled your lungs. For thirty years, you've been shouting yourself hoarse to the point where I don't understand how you still have a voice at all. Thirty years of refusing to have fun in the evenings because you have papers to grade and things to write instead, working by kerosene lamp until your eyes can no longer see. Thirty years now. I'm pretty sure it's no longer blood that flows in your veins, but red ink. Your entire life you've put all your strength and vitality into serving children. Now you have earned the right to take a rest. You have done more than enough for the country, and the country now has to compensate you, as you deserve. And besides, you can't even call it compensation. Not at all. A pension isn't a privilege but a right. You have served the nation, and the nation in turn shows its gratitude by giving back what it owes you. That's the least they can do. All these years they have taken a certain amount of money out of your salary. Now they will give it back to you. It's your money. It's the sweat off your brow. The gods and the ancestors don't even need to be with you in order to recover what is rightfully yours. The gods have no bearing in a state governed by the rule of law. You have carried out a job well done. Now go get what's coming to you."

During her rant the veins of her neck occasionally bulged out while the ones in her temples visibly throbbed. Decked out in a scarf, her head nodded defiantly. From the austere and contemptuous expression of her temper, one knew immediately that this mature woman commanded respect. After saying everything she had to say, her eyes rolled back in her head for a fraction of a second, her forehead crumpled with rage, her nostrils flared, and her mouth seemed to close definitively, exhibiting a frown of disgust. To conclude, she gazed purposefully outside at the *atangatiers* that the windows had framed as if they were a living portrait.

What hustle and bustle on the day Obame was to leave! The men stopped by either to find out about the departure time or to inquire about the mode of transportation Obame was taking. The women flocked to the kitchen to help Awu prepare for her husband's trip as she catered to his every need. She had washed, starched, and ironed his best shirts along with his handkerchiefs that she had embroidered herself. His old shoes were so carefully polished that they shone like new. Awu had prepared several dishes: smoked fish packed in cucumber seed, shrimp in peanut sauce, a few sticks of manioc, some bits of sweet banana, and some roasted peanuts. All of these foods could remain fresh for several days. And that was good because Obame was undertaking quite a long trip. First of all, he had to take a local bus from the village to the bus station in the city, and from there he had to catch yet another bus to the capital. At the very least, the trip would take a day and a half if the roads didn't present any hazards and provided that the bus was in good condition. During rainy season, it wasn't unheard of for that trip to last three days. And as a matter of fact, it was the rainy season. One had to prepare accordingly.

AWU AND NTSAME TOOK EVERY PRECAUTION IN HELPING ADA out of the bus; the bumpy race to the hospital had come to an end, with the driver slamming on the brakes so hard that it's surprising that the baby wasn't born on the spot. The abrupt halt had caused everyone to scream except for Ada who, already moaning for nearly an hour, had bit her bottom lip so hard that it bled.

The three women headed off on foot toward the provincial hospital that was visible from the bus station. Making it to just about fifty meters outside the main entrance, they were forced to slow their pace at the sight of a pack of dogs emerging from the shadows of one of the bunches of banana trees lining the road; the dogs were already ferociously tearing apart a burgundy-colored mass of flesh of some sort. As the three women approached the hospital, they were nauseated by the foul odor of decomposing meat while all the while the leaves and branches of the banana trees swayed to the calm and peaceful rhythm of a gentle breeze. Suddenly and quite brutally, they discovered the origin of the odor as they passed through the main entrance; sickly colored batches of gauze and cotton had been piling up and stuck at the bottom of two posts of an older-style stationary gate that stood just behind the outer wall. Seeing all of these tainted hues for a mere fraction of a second was more than enough to make an indelible mark on their memory: the blackish red of old, dried-up blood, tinges of dark red blood, the brownish red of festering blood, and reddish, whitish, milky pus. No longer startled by intruders passing by, flies were trying desperately to extract all that they could from these materials before the expert tongues of the neighborhood cats could get to them at the end of the evening.

Awu had given birth to her five children at the Ebomane clinic, which had closed a few months back due to a lack of medications. However, Awu knew the provincial hospital very well for some time now, or more precisely, ever since her husband had taken his retirement. Every month she would make a trip to the administrative center close by to sell her placemats to the public officials and to the wives of other prominent people in Ebiraneville.

As Ada's moans had cranked up a notch, Awu separated herself from their little group and at a pace somewhere between walking and running, she headed off in the direction of the maternity ward to let the midwife know they were coming. She knocked at the door and entered without waiting for anyone to open the door. She was surprised at how warm the midwife's greeting was in return. With a little more confidence, Awu proceeded inside the room, the two other women following close behind. After spotting Ada, the midwife asked her to produce her medical file. Ada promptly granted her request. The midwife took the file and said that only one relative at a time could remain in the delivery room. This was fine with Ntsame who, when it came right down to it, was a very squeamish person who could easily faint at the sight of blood. So rather instinctively, she left. The midwife closed the door behind Ntsame and casually asked Ada to hand over her surgical glove before lying on the delivery room table. Ada and Awu looked at each other perplexedly.

"What's a surgical glove?" asked Awu.

"What's a surgical glove? Why, it's the plastic glove we use for the examination!"

"No, we don't have that," said Awu dumbfoundedly.

"And thread? You have that, don't you?"

"Thread?" Awu resumed.

"Yes, the thread to tie up the cord!"

"The umbilical cord?"

"Well, I never! What other cord can I possibly be talking about?"

"No, we don't have that either," answered Awu mechanically.

"And of course you don't have a razor blade either."

"Razor blade?" Awu couldn't resist saying.

"Well, come on now! How are we supposed to cut the cord?" the midwife exploded.

"But we didn't know all of this, m'am! At other places . . ."

"At other places what? At other places what? Everyone tells me: 'At other places, at other places, at other places!' And then what! Do you think maybe I don't know what goes on at other places? Do you think I'm having fun helping women give birth on my measly salary? This time I've had it, and you're not getting away with playing this game with me. And besides, I don't even have five francs to my name. My own children didn't even eat last night. They only drank citrus juice, and without sugar at that. Meanwhile, I know that 'at other places' kids are stuffing themselves with good things to eat."

Just as she finished these words, Ada let out a piercing cry and began panting heavily. The midwife bent over her, tapped Ada's swollen stomach, and said to Awu:

"Obviously, she won't give birth for at least thirty more minutes. You have time to go down to the stand run by the Malian, the one located near the main entrance, just five minutes away. He has everything you need except for the surgical glove. In its place, you can buy two plastic bags—you know, like the ones used for wrapping things up. That's how we do the job for women who come with no surgical glove."

Awu went out and commissioned Ntsame, who came back a few minutes later with the requested items.

Ada was lying on the delivery room table. She tugged nervously on the mattress covered with a filthy plastic-coated canvas. And when the pain became unbearable, she tried to muffle her scream.

"Push it out for me!" said the midwife. "Push! Push! Now stop! Don't push anymore. Don't push again until I tell you to, you got that? Don't come here acting like a child with me. You weren't acting like a child when you got yourself pregnant. You're about to give birth. You're about to be a mother. Take responsibility for that or else I'll knock you out! Come on now, push," she said to Ada, who once again started panting like a puppy. "Push, push! Harder, harder! Are you going to push or not? Push!!! Good, now stop. Catch your breath. Breathe in. There you go . . . and breathe out! That's it. Good. Okay, now you're going to push, you're going to push. Push, push!! Push, you imbecile! You're not helping your child any by crying like an idiot. Stop breathing and push!!! Come on! You have already dishonored your parents enough by getting knocked up at your age! Save face, at least, by being tough! Send this child out to us! If not, I'm going to smack you!"

Never having been naked in front of strangers before, let alone having been called out on her bad behavior, Ada burst out sobbing from shame as well as from pain. Just like a little child, she cried her eyes out—she cried so loudly in fact that she even worried the midwife who promptly slapped Ada with the back of her hand.

"Push, push, push! Stop breathing! Pretend you're constipated! Then push with all you've got. Come on! Go ahead, that's it! Push, push!!! There you go!"

Ada's final gut-wrenching scream preceded the first cry of her offspring. Awu stared at the plastic-bag-wrapped hands that were gliding precariously around a sticky little body. Soon the Malian merchant's dust-laden weaving thread was knotted around the umbilical cord, and the partly rusted razor blade separated the child from its mother. This is how Sikolo Ntok made his grand entrance into the world in a provincial hospital at the dawn of the twenty-first century. The name had been chosen a long time ago. Ada had told her two aunts that if she gave birth to a boy, she would name him after his uncle Obame Afane, whose first name was Sikolo.

"It's all up to you now. My job here is done," said the midwife after cleaning and dressing the child before handing him over to Awu. "Call your sister who is waiting outside," she added.

Awu was afraid to bring the baby out of the room, so she opened the door halfway with her free hand and called in Ntsame, who arrived right away to grab the baby. But by the time Awu turned around again, both women found themselves face-to-face with the midwife, who was holding a thick, red-wine-colored mass of flesh on a bloodied steel tray. Awu and Ntsame were taken aback.

"This is your daughter's placenta. Take it and throw it out."

Ntsame was secretly delighted to be holding the baby in her arms, as it served as an excellent excuse for not carrying out this dreaded task. When Awu had had her own children, her mother and mother-in-law had taken turns handling her placenta. She herself had never even set eyes on any one of them. She knew indeed that one day it would be her turn to do this. But she just didn't think it would be so soon. She wasn't fully prepared. Her first three children were boys, the oldest of whom hadn't even turned twenty yet. She knew indeed that she was the mother of all the daughters in the family. But at that very moment, what that role fully entailed seemed to catch her off guard. Nonetheless she had a clan to defend and a husband to honor. Wasn't her life supposed to be like a chain stitch? In that case, piercing the fabric was the necessary first step.

"Here, take it," said the midwife impatiently, brandishing the tray. "And don't forget to clean everything," she continued. "Remember, I told you that my job here is finished."

Then, turning around toward Ntsame, the midwife said, "There is blood everywhere. Set the baby down next to his mother and start cleaning. Hurry up—someone else is waiting outside."

Without a word, Ntsame obeyed the order. She went to give the baby to Ada, who was relatively calm since fortunately she wasn't suffering from any cramps, which for some women are more painful than the childbirth itself. As Ntsame approached, Ada detected that her aunt was rather shaken up by all that was going on. What's more, she was convinced that it was the first time in her life that her aunt didn't fight back. But what Ada didn't realize was that Ntsame loved her younger brother Obame Afane, and so everything that Obame Afane tolerated, so could she, and unconditionally at that. Ntsame supported Ada because she wanted to help her brother come out victorious. In Ntsame's mind, Akut no longer counted.

"Where is the mop?" asked the midwife.

"Oh, yeah, the mop, I was just going to ask you about that."

"You were going to ask *me?*" the midwife answered back.

Ntsame couldn't resist the temptation. A sixth sense just wouldn't let her do it. She pretended to look around before the midwife once again went on the attack:

"What about the broom?"

"Broom?" Ntsame repeated mechanically once again.

Ntsame's inquiring look infuriated the woman, who exploded once more:

"Just exactly what planet do you come from?"

"Good question," Ntsame snapped back. "Because I was just wondering myself what kind of place this is!"

"Well, then, I can tell you exactly what kind of place this is! You are at the Ebiraneville provincial maternity hospital! When your family member gives birth here, you bring with you everything that you need, and afterward, you clean up everything she has soiled—and fast—because others are waiting."

Pronouncing these words, she helped Ada and her son move to a bare, filthy sponge mattress that was resting on the ground against the back wall. All the beds in the one and only maternity ward were occupied.

Ntsame was wearing a three-piece outfit consisting of a camisole and two bands of fabric, with one band coming up from behind to form a wraparound skirt, while the other end was attached fashionably haphazardly above the waist. She untied the one end and proceeded to wipe off the laminated surface of the birthing table by first dampening each corner of fabric with the water from the running faucet. While Ntsame was still meticulously engrossed in this task, Awu had returned with a defeated look and muddied hands. She went directly to the faucet which, of course, was still running.

"Don't bother washing your hands; you're not done yet," shouted the midwife, who was now busy trying to prepare a syringe. "You still have to clean the floor!"

Awu was wearing a large kaba. But as they had left Ebomane at an early hour, she had covered her shoulders with a long pagne. But as the temperature rose, she had attached the pagne around her waist.

At that moment she undid it, wet it, and threw it to the ground before crouching down and scrubbing the floor covered with tiny beige tiles that were actually more pinkish in certain spots than in others. She discovered, in fact, that washing the floor meant making all the bright red patches pink. It was quite difficult to determine precisely the original color of these tiles anyway because those around the sink were turning green due to the mold that was proliferating in that area. And near the entryway, the tiles were almost brown because of an endless cycle—mud had been tracked in, eventually turning into dust only to be transformed once more into mud.

Finally deeming the room suitable for receiving a new patient, the midwife released the two women from this ordeal. They went to wash their hands. The water pressure was too weak to allow the women to wash their pagnes as necessary. After a quick conversation, it was decided that Ntsame would go back to the village to wash the dirty laundry and to bring back food while Awu would stay to keep an eye on Ada.

Later in the night, curled up on the floor in the corner right next to Ada, Awu relived the scene in her mind once more, as if in a state of dreaming, as she stood outside the door of the maternity hospital in the face of the unknown, holding in her two hands the stained steel tray on which the mass of flesh was resting. Her confused look had caught the attention of an elderly woman sitting on the ground under the veranda, caressing the head of woman with a protruding belly; she was resting her head on the old woman's thighs, and the rest of her body lay stretched out on a pagne.

"My daughter," said the old woman, "how is it going?"

Awa was startled but did not answer. She was ashamed of admitting her inexperience, as that would have easily been interpreted as a sign of incompetence. She simply looked back at the woman, pretending as if she were in the know.

"I see," the woman said, raising her head in such a way that allowed her to look at Awu face to face. "Listen, my daughter, it's no big deal. You are in the city and you'll do like everyone else. You aren't going to keep this placenta until you return to the village, I hope! That child was born in the city. And this Mass of Life must fertilize the city. Take a machete from my sack over there. Follow the road and you will see clumps of banana trees off to the side. Choose yourself a nice spot and you bury it, your placenta. And don't forget the next time you come here, try to bring your own machete along with the baby's things."

THE TRIP WAS LONG BUT BEARABLE. ONCE IN THE CAPITAL, OBAME found a taxi driver to whom he dictated the address of a relative, the husband of his first cousin. He wasn't aware of any other close family members in Meyos.

He was warmly received. Salutations were brief, however. Everyone was in a hurry to leave, the little ones off to school and the adults to their jobs. Starting tomorrow, though, his in-law could accompany him to all the offices where he needed to go.

Almost every day at noon, when he would return with his cousin's husband from these appointments, he would find at the house relatives who had been informed of his arrival and knew of the purpose of his stay. Immediately after each welcome and without any lag time in between, they would subject him to their own problems. They thought that he had already received his pension, and each one was asking for a certain amount to support his own needs. He had lost touch with his oldest relatives a long time ago, and as for the younger ones, he barely recognized them and some, not at all. He told them that he hadn't received anything yet and that his file was still pending. It would have been nice to be invited over by any one of them. Even one time—just to get to know the family better. But this was not the case. He started to believe that everyone there had found an excuse for coming precisely at noon; although his cousin had prepared a hearty meal, the sheer number of unexpected guests spread lunch rather thin.

After four days he had accomplished all the necessary steps. He just needed two more documents that he would mail to his cousin's husband as soon as he got back to the village. After that, he would only have to wait for official notification from the Public Revenue Office.

After a week he returned home, happy to have discovered the capital. He was also glad to have reconnected with the family, but he was worried that they were all counting on him too much.

Upon his return he was warmly received as he told the village all about his stay. Many expressed their disappointment about all the hassles one must go through just to claim one's due. They figured it should more than suffice to simply report where one has worked and for how long, or if not, they thought administrative officials should be sent out to help all the government workers nearing retirement so that they could fill out these forms locally on the spot.

One month went by, then three, then seven! Still no notification, even though Obame mailed the missing documents as soon as he arrived home. And his cousin's husband even went to the trouble of dropping them off as soon as he received them. Obame Afane had to once again inquire by mail to know the exact reasons for this endless wait. He didn't want to make yet another trip to the capital unless he could be absolutely certain to bring back at least an advance on his pension if not the full benefits he should have already earned. Finally he received an official letter from the National Social Security Office asking him to come sign an additional document.

SINCE HER MARRIAGE AWU ENJOYED THE SOCIAL LIFE SHE HAD always dreamed of. Accompanied by her husband, she regularly visited the village for weddings, funerals, and other events. She was admired, respected, and asked for advice, even by elders. And she helped everyone the best that she could without a bit of arrogance. She was both proud and grateful when her husband would regularly send her family a sack of rice, kilos of beef, or pagnes.

This is the life they had both been used to up until his retirement. But now the good old days were over. Fortunately, her husband had already secured a certain social standing. He was revered and respected, mostly because of his honesty and generosity. Awudabiran' thought so highly of him and loved him just as much. But since his retirement she actually felt sorry for him, since his meager donations to various ceremonies organized either by his in-laws or his own family caused him to lose face little by little. But the fact that he was residing in a never-ending construction project was a dead giveaway as to what his true financial situation was. He couldn't take the gaping holes in his new home anymore.

What no one realized was that the family of Awudabiran' continued to receive their son-in-law's attention without him actually knowing it. Awudabiran' was determined to save face among members of her own family. And she was willing to pay the price. Her pride and love for her husband drove her to preserve the best possible image of their couple.

Since the start of Obame Afane's retirement, Awudabiran' was trying in every way imaginable to find extra work embroidering table linens. She made them for every taste and pocketbook. For those in the know, she was an expert of the art. Her work, in fact, demonstrated this talent. She feared that these same masterpieces were betraying her, revealing the unique pleasure she got from creating them as their sheer beauty spoke volumes. She and her works held many a secret!

If Awudabiran' hadn't had to help out Nguema Afane's two wives, who often had nothing to eat, and if she hadn't had full responsibility of Ada and her baby, her financial resources would have been sufficient. But given these circumstances, she had to learn how to cut down on expenses. In order to do this, she had to nix all luxury items including things like salt, peanut oil, bars of soap, kerosene lamps, and toilet paper. There weren't many residents in the village using these products anyway. Every kid in the village knew how to make salt from burning palm tree stumps. And gigantic clumps of palm trees proliferated along both banks and in forests. Peanut oil was expensive, but palm oil cost only the trouble of going to pick, boil, and grind the nuts. And those lumps of clay found either along the moist riverbanks or here and there in the underbrush—who wasn't aware of their value and their true properties for making skin softer? Earthworms manufactured these for free. And resin, this magic potion—has it not helped our eyes overcome darkness since the beginning of time?

As for toilet paper, was it all that necessary in the village? Why not make do like the villagers and use corncob hearts and malva leaves instead? Didn't Abi, Aladji the shopkeeper's wife, set aside a day when even she wouldn't use this paper she was selling? And in Awu's own culture, wasn't it customary just to rinse off with water? Why hadn't she maintained this custom? It's not like she hadn't tried. But she had done so only on occasion. And these occasions had always been very particular. In fact, the wc that housed the septic tank was the one and only place where it was possible to have any privacy. Its four walls made of tree bark and its little straw roof knew a thing or two about Awudabiran'. Hadn't these things witnessed each time she had squatted here contemplating using either the shelled corncobs or the malva stalks, everything arranged below her on a board covered in banana tree leaves? Ah, these walls of bark and the straw roof were the only confidantes she ever had; they knew very well that she found the corncobs more to her liking. It was a natural end for them, the end of a journey within all of creation. That which is born of the earth is finally returned to the earth. Those corncobs had no further use otherwise. It was a suitable destiny for them in their final stage of existence. It was more than adequate. It was why she preferred using them in that way, in spite of their roughness upon contact. In fact, each time she spotted those shelled corncobs, nothing about them reminded her of the tenderness of the once surrounding leaves or the smoothness of their stalk or the silkiness of the golden beard that had enveloped them. The multitude of empty sockets on these hollowed-out corncobs could only call to memory those fleshy kernels made to explode on contact with red-hot embers; kernels full of nectar from which one could prepare sweet and flavorful concoctions over a dying flame exuding an array of colors. After examining the naked corncob, she used it without any regret whatsoever, and it did the job with a delicate touch.

But it was a different story with the malva leaves. Each time that Awu had no choice but to use them, it would pain her nonetheless to soil these leaves of such a pure hue of green, although she had to admit that their softness was incredible. As much as she dreaded the thought of diminishing this true marvel of nature, she also looked forward to renewing the subtle pleasure of the velvety-smooth leaf caressing her skin.

WHEN ADA LOOKED AT HER BABY, YOU COULD SEE EVERYTHING on her face but a mother's love and tenderness. Awu had even noticed that Ada only held her child when it was time to breastfeed him. If he cried for any other reason besides being hungry, Ada didn't care. One day upon arriving home from work, Awu was alarmed by the child's shrill cries that could be heard from outside the house. She hastened her steps, thinking the baby must be alone and perhaps in danger. Much to her surprise, she found Ada and her two cousins sitting calmly in the living room conversing as if nothing were going on. Upon seeing their aunt, they were startled and immediately stopped talking. Ada got up and headed toward the bedroom, followed by Awu, who was in no mood to greet anyone. The toddler was lying on his back and screaming like the devil; on his little face, swollen and red, a combination of snot, saliva, tears, and sweat, and his feet wriggled about in the feces and urine in which his little bottom was also covered.

"*Akiééé*! Ada! *Akiéé*![1] Don't you get it that you are a woman now, that you're a mother, that this child is yours, and that you're the one responsible for him? Don't count on me for everything. Ada, make a bit of an effort! It's not normal how you are acting! It's not normal at all!"

In saying these words, she proceeded to put her purse on Ada's bed, took off her watch and placed it in her purse, and then removed her shoes. While this was going on, Ada grabbed the baby powder and a new change of clothes. Without any concern for her beautiful white percale dress with pink flowers, Awu took the baby in her arms and quickly exited the bedroom. Both of Ada's cousins were still in the living room. Awu ignored them as she went toward the bathroom where there was still a basin of clean water. The child had stopped crying but started to wail once again upon contact with the cold water. A moment later, one could hear him splashing about. Ada remained glued to the doorstep holding the baby powder and the baby's clothes. She was afraid of making eye contact with Awu, who was now sitting on a little bench allowing the baby to calm down by giving him a little fish to play with, one that Obame Afane had carved for him out of bamboo. The child desperately tried to submerge the fish, which kept popping up again to the surface. Ada ran up with a towel that Awu snatched out of her hands. She took the baby out of the water and brought him to the living room as Ada sheepishly followed behind. Awu sat down on the wood-trimmed couch and laid the baby out onto the towel. Both cousins remained silent, keeping a low profile. After having powdered and dressed him, Awu handed over the baby to his mother. It was at that very moment that Ntsame charged into the living room. She was holding a lovely basket with a handle. Her face became fraught with gloom at the sight of her two nephews sitting across the hallway; but then she lightened up once again seeing Ada take her child from Awu's arms.

"You look beautiful, my wife, in this pretty dress," said Ntsame, who often called Awu her wife.

As soon as Awu turned around toward her sister-in-law to greet her properly, Ntsame jumped back and said with a disgusted look:

"But, my word! You're covered in caca!" And turning toward Ada, she lashed out in a threatening voice:

"And where were you? Huh? You don't go to school anymore, and as for the child, you can't even take care of him! What exactly do you want to do what your life, huh? I'm asking you, what do you want to do? I bet these devils are responsible for corrupting you." She kept on turning toward her two nephews who, since their aunt's arrival, were trying to find a way to slip out without making it seem as if they were escaping.

"I told you they would be a bad influence on you! I bet you are neglecting this child because they've made you believe that it's Awu's job to take care of him! True or not? What an idiot! That way, if something happens to the child, everyone will blame Awu and say she's a bad woman. Let me tell you something, Ada. Awu can decide to never come near your child again if she wants. Your own mother abandoned you, and this is how you treat the one who took you in; by causing problems for her. You ingrate! Of course, you live under your uncle's roof, but you must know that Awu is under no obligation to do all that she does for you and your baby! Do you understand that? Huh? Do you understand? Yes or no?"

"Yes, Aunt Ntsame," Ada answered meekly.

The two cousins had gotten up and were about to slip out when Ntsame did an about-face, pointing her finger at them and saying:

"This is your fine work, I'm sure of it! You're corrupting this girl. And she's stupid enough to listen to you, to the point where she is risking the life of her own child. Aren't you ashamed at your age to be causing trouble like this all around you? What the heck happened to you at birth to explain how you've turned out this way? Don't you think Ada is messed up enough the way she is? Having a baby at the age of twelve, being abandoned by her mother and no longer in school—and to top it all off, you want to turn her into a criminal now! Is that it? In that way, perhaps she'll beat you at your own game one day. Admit it! But just let me tell you one last thing. In case you didn't already know it, you are pure evil! Now get out of here!"

Without further delay, the two finally managed to vacate the premises. Ntsame followed them out with her eyes, smirking as she saw them hightail it out of there once past the *atangatier*. When she turned to come back inside the house, Ada was breastfeeding her baby. Tears rolled down her cheeks and off of her chin before plopping down either on the baby's tiny hands or on his powdered little stomach.

"Don't cry while breastfeeding; it brings misfortune!" said Ntsame in a firm voice. "You're causing your child a stream of bad luck. Get a hold of yourself. It's never too late to do better. Life can still be good to you if you choose the right path. Starting now. Do you understand?

You're letting yourself go and that's not good. It's thanks to Awu's watchful eye that she and I know that you have developed an infection. It's easy enough to treat if it's caught early on. Your mother refused to let Awu pick some *zom ayo* leaves.[2] They are growing in abundance behind her house. And she's the only one who has any. Your Aunt Awu told her it was to treat you, her own daughter, but all in vain; that didn't change a thing. She even said that if Awu touched one single leaf in her garden, she would make her eat it before allowing her to leave. And since your Aunt Awu doesn't like trouble, she came to talk to me about it. I went immediately to your mother's house and I helped myself right before her very eyes without a hello or goodbye. Here are the leaves."

She took from her basket a bunch of thick, kidney-shaped leaves, so fresh that there were a few transparent, sticky droplets still left behind on their stalks. She handed the leaves over to Awu, who immediately began to select the best ones. When Ntsame finally decided to sit down, she said to Ada in a firm tone:

"You are going to follow your Aunt Awu's instructions to the letter. Negligence can make things go from bad to worse, making a mountain out of a mole hill. Do you understand what I'm telling you?"

"Yes, Aunt Ntsame," said Ada continuing to wipe away her tears.

"Is he satisfied now?"

"Yes, Aunt, he's full."

"Well, then bring the little rascal over to me . . . Oh! Would you look at that lively expression. That's a sure sign of intelligence! No, no, don't take off my scarf. I know you want to make fun of all my gray hair! You'll see one day when your wife is my age! If you break my necklace, I'll have to take all of your wife's jewels . . . Look what you've done to my beautiful pagne! Can you buy me another one? If you poke my eye out, you'll have to marry me . . . Oh, what an old man! He doesn't even have any teeth . . . Look! I have all of mine . . . not a single one missing . . . I'm just a young girl, in fact! Oh! Let's see these little feet that love kicking me in the stomach . . . Ah, look how smooth they are! Ah, yes they are! Oh! Just look at that! He can't stop laughing! He can't stop laughing! Don't you know that any self-respecting man shouldn't laugh like that? Come on now, show a little self-control! Okay, let's quit now before someone catches you in the act . . . it's not very manly, you know, and you'll be the laughing stock of the village! And no girl will want to marry you! All that will be left are old women just like me but with no teeth! Is that what you deserve, huh? Is that what you really deserve? Oh boy! And he's very ticklish on his stomach! What force! What a strong boy! Here, Ada, put him to bed. He should get some rest! See you later, young man, and don't forget that you still owe me a new pagne!"

Ada came to take the child and rushed off to his room.

"As you can tell," said Awu, folding the leaves briskly into a white enameled basin, "that baby is irresistible. Really, I can't understand how Ada can neglect him to the point where she would let him die if no one came to his rescue. You know, Ntsame, sometimes I think that Nguema Afane's sons have nothing to do with this whole affair. It must go much deeper than that, but we have no way of knowing anything more."

"We'll know one day," said Ntsame thoughtfully.

THE THOUGHT OF A SECOND COSTLY AND FRUITLESS TRIP TO THE capital really bothered Obame Afane. The village was indeed sympathetic. However, some were starting to believe that he would never see his pension. It got to the point where the Council of Elders asked Obame to consult a *nganga*3 in the hopes of destroying all the obstacles blocking this pension. The elders thought that the villagers' blind trust in the white man's system must have offended gods and ancestors alike who had been much too forgotten in this whole affair. Thus they had to be asked for forgiveness and for their blessing. They had shown that the village couldn't go on without them.

It would be easy if all Obame would have to do is consult a nganga. The real problem was that he simply didn't believe in them anymore. Did this nganga manage to make his land fertile some time ago? He would never forget that . . . .

Nonetheless he eventually gave in and did what the Elders wanted.

In order to pay for this second trip, Obame had to get a loan from one of the teachers who was still working. The fact that this teacher was an old friend of Obame didn't prevent him from feeling mortified. Nor did Awu feel any less humiliated. But she was determined. The time had not yet come for her to reveal her big secret.

Obame made the thirty-six-hour trip to affix his famous signature. Luck seemed to finally be on his side; at the Bureau of Public Revenue, an officer informed him that he could start collecting his benefits the very next day. He returned to his relative's house in disbelief. However, he told himself that he was ready to spend the entire next day downtown if necessary. But when Obame arrived at his relative's house that evening, he was told that tomorrow was just decreed a holiday; the *fête du mouton*.⁴ As he was not in a celebratory mood, he made up a story that while running his errands, he had bumped into an old friend who invited him over to his house. Then the next day, Obame took a taxi and got out just a few hundred meters away. He wandered in the streets of the capital for a few hours just to pass the time—and to let off some steam. As for his lunch, he bought himself a little carton of sweet condensed milk that he broke open with his pocketknife. After looking around to make sure no one was watching, he drank it inconspicuously as he continued wandering. He walked around until evening. When his feet started to drag, he headed back toward the house.

The next day, there were huge lines at the cashier's office; the collection office's payment schedule was indeed set, but there weren't any more available funds in the revenue office. He would have to wait a few more weeks before getting paid.

He went back home to the village more disappointed than ever and decided, among other things, that he no longer wanted to hear another word about this nganga.

The trip back was particularly treacherous because of all the dust. It was the dry season, and all along the route Mother Nature, donning her ruby dress, covered herself in a fine red powder to complete her look. With no more spare change to take the bus, Obame Afane the schoolteacher walked from the bus station to the village. This time he wasn't even able to bring back a single spool of thread for his wife. He was exhausted and completely covered in dust. Upon seeing him, all of the children in the village, including his own, started shrieking with joy and greeting him warmly. But it was clearly a dejected man who slowly made his way across the village. Once she saw him coming, Awu gently closed the mahogany doors and windows and stood in front of the door. Then she let her husband come to her, his ruby-colored clothes and all. When he was just a few steps away from his home he finally realized what was going on and stopped in his tracks—petrified and awestruck—and his mood completely changed.

Awu turned around to open the door. She entered and gracefully opened the shutters of the courtyard windows. Then she stood in the middle of the room across from the entryway, leaning against a large table also made of mahogany. Her ruby husband finally came into the house. He walked slowly toward her. When he was a couple of steps away, he stopped and muttered:

"Awu, what did you do here? Your money is for you and your parents; especially now that I can no longer send them anything. What have you done?"

"I can't rightfully take care of my parents if my own situation here is in need of attention."

"But did you realize that by doing this, the whole village will think it's you who is supporting us? That it's you, the head of the family? That it's you, the man of the house? Do you really think that I can tolerate such a thing?"

"But how will anyone know? They'll think that perhaps you had put some money away on the side! I told Mezui Mba that you were the one who sent me. Even the children think that you paid for these windows. What good is it to be married if we don't share any secrets? It's true. Between you and me, we don't have any real secrets."

"Okay, this will be our secret. Although as soon as I get my pension, I'm paying you back for everything. Okay?"

"Okay, if that's what you really want."

"So then . . . hello."

And he took his wife by the shoulders and drew her close to him. She gently removed her husband's arms, placing them instead around her waist. She then whispered:

"If you are really the head of this household, then break me in two. If you have it in you, that is. That's what I want. Squeeze me. Tight."

And he squeezed her. Tight. Really tight.

When he felt that she was about to faint, he loosened his embrace. She propped herself up against the table. He pulled up two chairs and they sat down. Outside, the children were singing cheerful songs. Obame devoured his wife with his eyes as he had never done before.

Still a bit out of breath, Awu looked down. She wanted to stop time at that very moment, her husband looking so intently at her, just like in her fantasies.

"I had forgotten that I am not so young anymore," she said finally looking up.

They smiled, looking at each other with tenderness.

A YEAR AFTER OBAME AFANE'S SECOND TRIP, HIS COUSIN'S HUS-
band sent him a letter from the capital informing him that his
retirement file had been lost. While going to check on the progress
of the file, his relative was told by the officers that there was no trace
of it in their records and that they didn't have the time to dig through
the mountains of paperwork; thus, it was best to start over again from
scratch. His cousin's husband even pointed out how he had made
quite a scene in the office where the file was supposed to have ended
up, but there was nothing that could be done.

More than ever the chain stitch represented love and life for Awu-
sdabiran'. She was secretly proud of all of the ringlets that she had
carefully crafted throughout the course of her life: her studies, her
career, her marriage, her children, her showing of generosity toward
her family and her in-laws. Her modesty and extreme discretion had
paid off in that she never had any overt conflict with anyone. But
just being beautiful and brilliant alone was cause for some, on the
other hand, to have an unfavorable impression of her and, in fact,
it even incited jealousy. But she pretended not to notice. To make a
chain stitch, don't you have to first start from the back and, before
you pull the needle through, you have to slide the thread through the
head of the needle? Wasn't this the stipulation for pulling the needle
through so that a pretty little ring would be left behind on the fabric?
This thread, so meek in appearance, ends up imposing its splendid
beauty, commanding respect and admiration.

Ever since her husband had allowed her to contribute to the financial
needs of their household, Awu appeared more considerate and more

loving than ever. She knew that her husband suffered deeply from his humiliating situation. She tried to lift his spirits. But she simply couldn't find the right words. So instead she became noticeably more daring in her intimate relationship with her husband. One evening, as they were lying like a needle and thread ready to form rings, she announced to him:

"Do you know that the two of us have never made love together?"

Obame said nothing as if he had always known that this question would come up one day.

Awu continued:

"It's true, after almost twenty years of marriage, we've never made love. Each time you've embraced me, I have never really felt you with me; I've been a replacement. One time you even murmured in your sleep, 'Bella!' and you started sobbing in this state of delirium. I tapped your shoulder and you calmed down. How you must have loved Bella! We are kind of the same, you and I, do you know that? Because when you hold me, I imagine myself with someone else, just for my own peace of mind. And I imagine that my lover's body and mine recognize each other in ecstasy, two kindred spirits. And this imaginary lover has really developed in my mind, just like Bella has invaded yours. The result is that both of us are left unsatisfied since each of us is chasing a phantom. But you do know that I don't blame you at all, don't you? How could I? Who can control love? Maybe if Bella hadn't died in such cruel and unjust circumstances, your heart wouldn't be so heavy. So refusing to give your body and soul to any other woman is your way of rebelling, of avenging her death, of staying faithful to her. I understand all of that. And what about you? I hope you don't hold it against me to have cheated on you with the image of this man stuck in my head?"

"Oh, no, Awu, no," Obame finally said. "The only thing I can fault you for is your perfection! You are a true angel! How can one person have as many qualities as you do?"

"By sewing my life together as a series of chain stitches."

"Huh?"

"Oh, nothing, just thinking aloud."

"And since we are thinking aloud, it's my turn now to admit something to you; this is maybe the first time you and I are speaking about Bella, but it's really the very first time that someone besides my sister Ntsame understands the extent of my sorrow and can find a justification for it. And it's precisely you, my wife, who has helped me to heal my bleeding heart. Oh, Awu! You have managed to connect with me somehow. You have just reached the innermost depths of my soul . . . And you will remain in my heart forever. I am no longer alone. Thank you, my wife. Thank you, my sister. Thank you, my beloved. And I'm going to prove to you that there are no more secrets between us, except for the ones we share."

Then, still in a lying position, he reached up toward the solid wood headboard and effortlessly slid open a crosspiece revealing a little machete lodged in the pit of the wood, its blade as straight and gleaming as a ray of sunshine.

"Hey! What's that?" said Awu, taken aback.

"That's me," answered Obame mysteriously, extracting the knife from its hiding place. "It's the knife that separated me from my mother at birth. My grandmother gave it to me when I was a child so that I can remember."

"Remember what?"

"Them!"

"What do you mean? The family? Who forgets their family? I don't get it."

"No, she wasn't afraid I would forget them. She just wanted me to always remember."

"And what's the difference?"

"There isn't any, except for this machete. My grandmother never went to school so she let objects 'speak' for her. Look at this knife. She used it. When she cut the umbilical cord, one side of the blade was facing me and the other side, naturally, was facing my mother. The same knife that separated me from my mother also united us. She represents all our ancestry and I the next generation. But we are one because of our lineage, just like the two sides of this blade belong to the same knife. My grandmother gave it to me so that I can make sure my descendants follow the right path. She had absolute confidence in me. I don't know if I deserve it! I don't know if I'm cut out for such a mission. There are so many things I can't control. I also want to admit to you that on more than one occasion, I thought about committing suicide because of all the trials that this inaccessible retirement pension has made me endure. But the presence of this object is there to reassure me each time I lose faith. Well, there you have it. Now you know my secret!"

Awu took the knife out of her husband's hands, touched the blade in admiration, and then put it delicately back into place. Effortlessly, she closed the crosspiece. The headboard once again took on its ordinary appearance.

"No," said Awu turning toward her husband, "it's no longer your secret but our secret."

"And now," whispered Obame pulling his wife against him, "I have work to do. I've got to try and dislodge a certain guy from my wife's head."

OBAME AFANE HAD INDEED COMPLETED A NEW FILE DURING A third trip to the capital. Exactly two years later, the long-awaited notice finally arrived. The pension was ready. He would even get back pay. Obame felt that this time it was for real.

He asked his wife to accompany him. She had never been to the capital before. And she had several table linens to sell. They would have a good time. Didn't they deserve it? Awu wanted her husband to believe that this was all his idea so she held back a bit before agreeing. But she was actually dying to go.

One more time, the village was abuzz. Awudabiran' was leaving for the capital with her husband. She was overjoyed but tried to appear indifferent in order not to bring bad luck upon them.

That morning she and her husband took a longer swim than usual.

The big bunches of banana trees spread out on both sides of the road leading to the village always had a profound effect on Obame Afane, but this time they moved him in a different way, although he wasn't quite sure why. All along his route they seemed to stand in attention, as if they were giving him VIP treatment. The large leaves swayed gently to the rhythm of the morning breeze as if whispering a lullaby. The foliage glistened with thousands of droplets of fine mist. The soft earth gave way beneath him with each step. He thought he heard in the distance the echo of the name that his grandmother had given him. Sikolooo! Sikolooooo! However, he refrained from answering. But his heart started to beat like a *tam-tam*. He stopped and asked his wife:

"Awu, did you hear something?"

Awu then stopped as well, lending an ear with utmost concentration.

"No," she said, "I don't hear anything. I didn't hear a thing."
And they returned to the village in silence.

Komandé, the former police chief, always hoped that his pension would arrive sooner or later. After many years of waiting, his confidence and optimism remained unwavering. However, his financial situation was in constant decline to the point where he had been forced to resort to drastic measures of which he was not very proud.

In fact, he owned an old clunker of a car; anyone who laid eyes upon it would have thought that it wasn't capable of withstanding the smallest bump or any excess weight. When times were rough, he transported villagers to earn some spare change, barely making it from the bus station and back. He didn't have a fixed rate. Each person gave what he could. And most of the time, they couldn't give much. But Komandé didn't complain. It's certainly the reason why no one thought of turning him in for going to the highway at the entrance of the village dressed in his old, but well-ironed uniform to stop all of the truck drivers; those who weren't in compliance paid a fine on the spot. Each time he had a good day, the next day he would bring along villagers free of charge on his way to get gas or to run errands.

In spite of the fact Komandé did not formally believe in God, he refused nonetheless to resort to such activities on Sundays.

Although the route was dusty and the passengers would be packed tightly in the bus like sticks in bound bundles of wood, Awudabiran' put on her prettiest dress—a beautiful kaba in red cotton imprinted with big green leaves. She wore a matching scarf on her head with a touch of playfulness; she had raised the scarf at the nape of the neck, allowing two little braids to escape out on each side while a third in the middle stuck out onto her forehead, much like a fern leaf. The folds in her kaba started out tiny near her chest, gradually creating a graceful ripple-effect at the ankles. Obame was wearing his handsome, well-starched yellow dress shirt. It was a little worn out, but it was still decent. He was saving the nice white boubou that Awu had sewn for him for the capital. That is, once they dusted off and cleaned up. They both looked like newlyweds who had been prematurely projected into their future. They were a beautiful couple. They loved each other. And curiously, they were still flirtatious. In twenty years they had never taken a single long trip together. This was like the start of a new life for them. They made up their minds to live life together to the fullest—for themselves and for their children. They had come to an agreement. All this time lost. All this time spent taking care of others. The moment had finally come to think about themselves and to enjoy the good things in life together, because there were certainly good things ahead. And the retirement pension was one of them.

PART **THREE**

AFANE OBAME, THE FATHER, HAD LEFT HIS HOUSE EARLIER THAN usual. The village was still sleeping; here and there, the hens and their chicks were already on a quest for those late-night worms and the early-riser ants. Afane Obame had been wide awake all night long. His mind had been put on alert by the menacing song of the clairvoyant owl. As he was walking toward the *corps de garde*,[1] Afane Obame noticed an eerie patch of darkness chiseled into the bright early morning sky; the patch got bigger and bigger as it raced toward the earth at lightning speed. Its shape was becoming clearer; within a split second, the talons of a sparrow hawk closed in one of the chicks, lifting it off the ground. Afane Obame followed the bird with his eyes until its image shrank little by little, eventually evaporating into the vastness of the sky. He kept his eye on the heavens for a moment, then looked inquisitively and imploringly toward the summit of the Wood-Girded Hill. Finally, he went to take a seat in the corps de garde. The writing on the wall was clear.

It was no surprise to see Pastor Gambier coming up hurriedly from a distance. He was out of breath by the time he reached the corps de garde. He remained standing without saying a word, as if to catch his breath. Afane Obame looked at him calmly.

"Afane Obame," he finally said, "get up, we are going to pray."

"Are you out of your mind, Pastor? Do you realize that you are speaking to Afane Obame, the high priest of the Ancestors' religion, he who protects the Wood-Girded Hill? Because of your long robes, I never really considered you a man. But if you have come here to provoke me as such, we can go at it man to man! Don't expect to tarnish the memory of my Ancestors with such impunity!"

"I have to tell you something very important. And I can't tell you without first praying with you to Our Creator."

"Your creator, not mine! And if what you have to tell me is so important, you can go ahead and pray all by yourself! Or else, take your news with you, good or bad. You are the head of your flock. I'm the head of my flock. If you are moving the Wood-Girded Hill to put it next to the Cross-Topped Hill, come ask me again to come pray with you. But until then, you haven't said anything and I haven't heard anything."

Seeing that it was no use insisting, Pastor Gambier, still standing, closed his eyes and started to mutter a prayer. At the end of it, he opened his eyes once more and sat across from Afane Obame, who was looking off in the distance, in the direction of the Wood-Girded Hill.

"Obame Afane is dying," said the pastor as calm as he could be.

Afane Obame was startled. Then he jumped up into the air in a way no one would have ever thought possible for a man his age.

"Pastor, what are you saying?"

"Exactly what you heard. Your son Obame Afane is dying in a hospital in the capital, where he was transported along with his injured wife and all the other passengers of the bus involved in the accident. One of my parishioners was traveling with them, but he wasn't hurt. He gave the message to the new missionary, who arrived in Ebomane just a few minutes ago."

"Tséééééééééén! Oh, Pastor! Tsééééén!"[2]

The piercing cry shook the entire village. Men and women came running from all around, everyone asking the same questions:

"What is it? What's happening? What? Who died? What is this craziness?"

Meanwhile, Afane Obame sat back down, staring at the ground. The pastor, who was also sitting, remained silent. The villagers quietly and slowly came toward them with an inquisitive look and their mouths agape; they expected shocking news. The pastor got up again, but refrained from asking people to pray.

"Obame Afane has been in a very serious accident on the outskirts of the capital. He is in the hospital in critical condition. But nothing is impossible with God. So therefore, don't despair, my brothers! If I have come all this way, it's not only to bring you this sad news, but it's also to urge you to take action right away, to try to save our son and brother. Listen to me! Listen, my brothers! Obame Afane was transported to the hospital, but so far he hasn't received any care because he must first hand over a deposit of 50,000 CFA[3] before being operated on. His wife was able to put down a total of 30,000 CFA. She doesn't know the capital and doesn't know how to reach any family member living there. She is hospitalized as well, but in a less critical state than her husband. We have to find 20,000 CFA in a hurry, my brothers! Time is of the essence. The missionary is going back this evening. Today is Sunday. In a bit, I'm going to ask the faithful of my church to make a special donation during the regular collection. All together, we can do this. Between the two Hills, we must come up with the money before the sun sets!"

Ada, who was listening from afar, holding her child by the hand, let go of him suddenly; she thrashed about on the dusty ground, screaming like a possessed woman. The child started to cry. Without another word, Pastor Gambier went off in the direction of the Cross-Topped Hill, leaving the Wood-Girded Hill in shock.

Between both Hills the necessary amount had been raised, and Pastor Gambier gave the money to the missionary, who took off early afternoon in the church vehicle. He was delayed a few seconds by Komandé, who had flagged him down and was running toward him waving his arms, having just parked his old car off to the side of the road. The missionary waited for Komandé who, all out of breath, gave him a few coins and said to him in a broken voice:

"God will understand. This is for Sikolo Obame Afane."

That night, each of the two Hills made a plea for mercy to their respective God.

But neither one of them was victorious.

The writing on the wall was clear, even before the missionary left. The money arrived much too late.

BACK FROM THE BURIAL, AWU FELT THEM UNDRESSING HER. She was cold. They wrapped what felt like a worn-out pagne around her chest. They made her sit on the ground. Then she felt them shaving her head. She shivered at the sight of her doomed braids rolling off her naked shoulders and free-falling to the ground. But her shivering was neither from cold nor from anger. With her head lowered, she continued to endure the rest that was in store for her, just like a martyr.

Passively, she submitted to the ritual inflicted upon a widow by her in-laws and, in particular, by her sisters-in-law. Akut was at the head of the line. The hostilities started by Akut slapping Awu hard in the face:

"Just how proud are you now of your table linens and your thin waist?" she began before spitting in Awu's face. Awu was not allowed to wipe it off. "What does that make you now? A loser, doesn't it? Why didn't you die with your husband? Huh? It's not so you can hang around lending out your vagina to any man who comes along, enjoying my brother's possessions all by yourself ? Bring the hot pepper! Let's burn it a bit, this vagina that belonged to us; she'll waste no time letting others left and right have a piece of it! Is that what you call love? Don't you know that in some places, a woman who really loves her husband lets herself be buried alive right along with him?"

A woman brought over a little bottle containing a blackish mixture, and a stick had been plunged inside.

"All right now. Lie down and spread 'em . . . I mean, if you really loved your husband, that is!"

Like a robot, Awu lay down and complied. And at the very moment when Akut was getting ready to apply a dose of hot pepper in the most intimate part of her sister-in-law's body, a powerful voice made her freeze in her tracks.

"Akut, no! If you really loved your brother, for his sake, don't do this!"

"So, let her pay!" said Akut, clearly annoyed.

One of Awu's sisters sitting near her feverishly undid a knot from one end of her scarf, took a coin from it, and was ready to drop it in the basket reserved for this purpose since Awu had to pay in some way if she did not want to endure the physical abuse prescribed. But by paying, this also meant that the widow wasn't ready to make sacrifices for the person she loved.

"Wait, no! She has to pay the way I've said!" exclaimed Akut, not accepting the alternative. "Come on, open up! Perhaps deep down, you're gonna like it, a whore like you! Light-skinned women are such damn whores! Especially those with freckles, like you! Come on, take that!"

Without any reserve whatsoever, she drove in the stick and swirled it around in the Door of Life.

A loud and totally unexpected slap on the back startled Akut who got up once more, dropping the weapon she used to commit the crime. She turned around in order to identify the agent of this act and found an emotionless Ntsame who simply said to her:

"You are the absolute last person who should be doing this."

Awu was sweating profusely, shaking with pain, her teeth and fists clenched to prevent her from screaming.

Akut went to sit down, mumbling under her breath and ashamed because everyone knew her story.

Soon, another slap resounded, but this time it was between Awu's shoulder blades. She could tell who did it because of the voice. It was a sister-in-law from the village, just out for some fun:

"Take that for having taken advantage of my brother the way you did. You didn't even have a co-wife! You were housed like a queen in her castle . . . with windows and doors made of solid wood! Isn't that what your house is like? Huh? And all the while I, Obame's own sister, was living in a house made out of bark. What makes you more special than us that you deserve all that? Let's see how proud you are now! I hope that all these blows will bring down your ego a notch or two!"

For almost a week there was abuse after abuse. Awu got slapped for each and every gift she had ever received from her husband, and she paid for all the hearty laughter that had livened up her household during those happy times. She got kicked in the ribs for the beautiful table that had a place of honor in her home. She was elbowed in the back for having been the queen of the house. She received a torrent of abuse. She received a torrent of insults. On several occasions she had to pay for merely surviving her husband. Awu's mother constantly kept urging her daughter to endure because, as she kept saying, by obediently subjecting herself to all of these ordeals, Awu would bring honor not only to her family but also to the memory of her late husband. She had even told Awu that she should consider herself lucky to be the object of such unrelenting punishment, since after the period of mourning had passed, a widow would surely find serenity once again. But if the widow refused to submit to the ritual or if, for some reason or another, her in-laws decided not to subject her to it, she would be considered condemned—not to death—but to insanity. To sum it up, submitting to this ritual drove away evil and appeased the spirit of the dead spouse.

Surrounded by her sisters and friends who had come to help her, Awu slept on the ground for seven days. Seven days during which it was forbidden for her to raise her head, to speak, to eat without permission, or to wash.

Finally, it was the last night of the ritual that Awu would spend on the ground. Having trouble containing her hatred, Akut wanted to try one last torment, sticking her index and middle fingers into Awu's nostrils while forbidding her from opening her mouth—all this just so Awu could prove that she had really loved her husband. After a few long seconds without taking a breath, Awu's veins began to bulge out of her temples and neck and Ntsame intervened once again. As she pulled her fingers out, Akut showered her in a hail of spit that eventually mixed with Awu's own tears and snot. With a voice emitting a combination of fear and anger, Ada exploded:

"Yes, mother, Aunt Ntsame is right. I will go so far as to say that it isn't only in memory of Uncle Sikolo Obame Afane that you should leave Aunt Awu alone, but it is to honor her as well because of all that she has done for me, your only daughter, and for your grandson, my child, Sikolo Ntok. You can't even hold a candle to this woman on whom you have just spit. I will no longer keep silent, Mother. I've remained silent for too long. You always find yourself on the wrong side in situations like this because you always make bad choices. This woman means everything to me, your own flesh and blood. You are trying to perpetuate the same kind of injustice that took Uncle Obame Afane away from us. Instead of attempting to find out what had really happened to me, you sent me away and abandoned me. You never even asked me how I had gotten pregnant, but now I'm going to tell you how. You got rid of me by sending me away to boarding school so that you could go about your business. But the people in charge there have no morals at all and take advantage of students, especially those like me, whose parents never visit them nor provide money for their everyday needs. I have at least five witnesses here in this room. Do you want to know what the people in charge at the Mbiosi boarding school subject us to? The school monitors ask us for two cigarettes for each hour we are absent. In order to get a passing grade on an assignment, students whose mothers sell palm wine must provide the teacher with a bottle. Good student or not, to ensure a passing grade in a subject for the three trimesters, you have to pay 15,000 CFA to the teacher or, if not, prepare to give him three sessions of gratification."

A young man came up, yelling at the top of his lungs:

"And do you want to hear what happens to male students who are poor? Well, we have to provide the teacher with a sister! And if we don't have one, we will bartend for the teacher's wife every night for a month! And if the teacher's wife has no bar, he uses you like a woman! My guy friends tell me that they aren't even sure they can have children later on after everything the teacher has done to them."

"And to be promoted on to the next year," Ada continued, "you just have to accept to be the teacher's mistress for the whole year! And you can't even go turn the teacher in to the principal because he himself is leading this pack of these dogs! That's why I hate my child! He has the face of his fifty-something-year-old father! I would have indeed had an abortion, but my thirteen-year-old classmate died the month before I got pregnant. She had tried to abort all on her own. I was afraid so I kept my baby. During the whole pregnancy, I secretly hoped my child would be stillborn; unfortunately, the bad seed is always the toughest one to get rid of. The proof of this reality is that Uncle Obame, the spiritual father of all the students and the exemplary schoolteacher, is the one six feet under today, without ever having been compensated for his devotion or for the goodness of his soul. This must not bother you too much, Mother, because in a sense, you are delivering a similar unjust destiny to Aunt Awu. Today you are teaming up with Aunt Ekobekobe, whom you have always detested, because her only purpose in life is to gossip, and you have often been her victim. So your lifelong enemy has come here to beat up on the wife of your biological brother and you're fine with that—you don't even give it a second thought. If there are people who warrant punishment here, it's indeed you and her; you are unworthy of being a mother!"

As Ntsame was overwhelmed emotionally with the gravity of all these revelations, she had to sit down, and did so robotically on a bench at the other end of the room across from Awu. And even though Awu was still keeping her head down, the two women still managed to exchange glances; this only lasted a fraction of a second, but that's all it took to acknowledge they had discovered the missing piece of the puzzle.

After finishing her story, Ada began to cry hysterically. Her peers came to be by her side before taking her outside to calm her down. Akut said nothing, but Ekobekobe gathered her things in an obvious manner and took off toward the door, railing against the younger generation who insisted on distinguishing between biological siblings and others.

The night would be short because very early in the morning, Awu would be released after submitting to a final series of trials concerning the maternal uncles of her husband. She was to cook a generous amount of *nteteghe*: a well-prepared dish whose degree of succulence was supposed to equal the amount of love Awu had for her husband. It was not only a dish made with love but also a farewell dish of sorts, as the maternal uncles would be eating hers for the last time as a tribute to their deceased nephew.

But the very last test would prove to be the hardest of all for her: she was supposed to publicly declare how many times she had committed adultery and with whom. Then she was supposed to pay a certain sum for each unfaithful act committed. But even if she had never been guilty of adultery, she was supposed to pay nonetheless so as to not give the impression that she was an undesirable woman, which in itself could also be perceived as a source of shame for the husband and the clan alike. So she was accused of this offense. And she paid.

FINALLY, AWU ONCE AGAIN HAD THE RIGHT TO GO ABOUT HER daily business, and when she entered her bedroom for the first time— the one she had shared with her husband—she realized that it was nearly empty. Everything had been taken, even her clothing. Her dishes and all her kitchenware had disappeared. Practically nothing was left from all that they had brought out for the reception. Her sister, who arrived the same day as the burial, told her how she had witnessed the dishes steadily diminish in number before, during, and after the meal. For the most part friends and relatives who came from the village, as well as those who had come from elsewhere, sought to walk away with something. Several cooking pots that were missing had disappeared with all the food still inside, this before anyone had even had the chance to eat from them.

But in spite of everything, the funeral had been a success. A representative from the National Ministry of Education had delivered a eulogy during which he denounced the injustice of the whole affair. Pastor Gambier praised the devotion of Obame Afane who, despite never having been baptized, had behaved like a true Christian his whole life. He had been the Good Samaritan who hailed from Ebomane. Pastor Gambier announced that Obame was looking down upon them at that very moment, already sitting in heaven at the right hand of the all-powerful God the Father. Ntsame came to criticize the ungrateful and inhumane administrative system that murdered her brother, with all its red tape that leads to nothing but misery and death. She concluded by letting her wish be known for an enlightened dictator to come to power in the not-so-distant future who would start off by administering a public lashing to all the lazy government workers before proceeding next to the execution of all leaders who have abused their authority along the way. As for Obame's father, he claimed to have always known that the proliferation of white education would sooner or later end up in the sacrifice of one of their own, and that Obame Afane was therefore doomed from the start. Wasn't he born the very day that the school opened? Hadn't he been named "Sikolo"? Afane Obame acknowledged that he had always known that his son didn't really belong to them; he had come among them to fulfill the mission of a schoolteacher, and he had left this earth once that mission had been accomplished. His just reward was not to be reaped here. His place was now at the peak of the Wood-Girded Hill among his brave ancestors, who held in their right hand a hunting weapon, vestige of their glorious past in this world full of obstacles. But unlike them, in his right hand, Obame Afane, the son, held a stylus, the weapon of his time.

Before the funeral Awudabiran' had given the organizers three-quarters of her savings as she had been warned that donations were minimal. She was determined to give her husband a decent funeral. And the organizers invested the entire sum in food and drink; the Protestant Mission offered to have the coffin made, and the arrangements for the final resting place had been taken care of by the school. No family member offered to take on these expenses. That was rather odd considering the flood of so-called relatives who showed up to eat and drink after the funeral. These same ones who had disappeared when they were really needed to organize a final send-off for their brother had now been the first ones to take advantage of a distant relation to get first crack at food and drinks.

Awu had been stripped of everything. But in any case, who really cared that she had nothing left? Wasn't she herself a thing? A possession? To prove it, after the funeral, the Family Council gave away all of schoolteacher Obame Afane's clothes—except for his underwear—to his maternal uncles. They then gave his gun to his oldest son. His books and his house were divided among all of his children. And as for Awu, she was bequeathed to Nguema Afane, the jobless bigamist who was living at the home of his own kids.

Awu had nothing left. She wasn't anything herself anymore. She didn't even want to think about what a court of a law would have determined for her case. She did know, however, that had she revealed her entire story, she indeed would have won her case. But the thought of letting people know just how much she contributed to the couple's wealth prevented her from going further. It was their secret alone. And in any case, she was far too much of a private person to do something like that. The memory of her husband had to be left unscathed. He was the man. And he had to remain a man in the eyes of everyone else. Forever.

And thus, she had the impression that her life had been sewn together by a chain stitch with no knot at the end. And just by chance, someone went and tugged on the thread. And everything was wiped out. She had nothing left except for the excruciating pain of three empty holes on the fabric, and this hurt so badly deep down inside her.

Two nights after the gathering of the Family Council, Nguema Afane entered Awu's bedroom without knocking. She was sitting on the edge of the bed. She was holding an open notebook in her left hand and was staring at it as if she had been hypnotized by it. And with her right index finger, she brushed the margin of a page where red marks had been scribbled; one would have said that she was trying to bring them to life. She didn't even flinch when Nguema Afane entered through the half-opened door. Without saying a word, he headed over toward the makeshift chair and dragged it over noisily, placing it right in front of Awu. It was at that moment that Awu finally snapped out of it; she jerked her head up and was dumbfounded to discover Nguema Afane sitting there. And as usual, he wasn't exactly sober. It's no wonder, considering the way he had been carrying on throughout the entire village about how a man's virility is measured by his capacity to gulp down as much alcohol as possible without really getting drunk.

"Aka!" Awu let out.

"It's only me," said Nguema Afane, calmly sitting down on Obame Afane's chair, a lugubrious smile on his face.

"You're just like your kids; ever since yesterday, they've been coming into my room whenever they want. The twins are having a hard time accepting that. If I hadn't been here, they would have beaten up your intruder of a son!"

"Intruder? My son? Did you just say 'intruder?'"

"Yes. In my room, I consider your son an intruder."

"Your room? You have a room here, you say? But you still don't get it yet that from now on, I am the head of the house here? You are a thing, and things don't acquire ownership. And moreover, you are my thing."

Awu was neither shocked nor saddened. She no longer had any feelings or emotions. But as firmly as possible, she responded:

"Nguema Afane, listen to what the Thing is going to tell you. Yes, custom has it . . . that is, the village has decided that I belong to you as part of the inheritance. Yes, it's true that you are the master of the house here because my children aren't yet adults. The thing that I am can do nothing against an entire community, against tradition. This is true. And I don't want to abandon my children or subject them to anything. But just look around you. Take a good look at this room. It's the room in which your brother and I lived. Of course, a good portion of the items from this room are now scattered throughout various houses of family members. But all the items that are here have seen me evolve with him. They know all my secrets and all those I shared with Obame Afane. So listen to me very carefully. Nguema Afane, all the items here are witnesses of what I'm going to say to you. It's the bedroom of secrets. I'm going to tell you a secret, and that will be our secret alone; I am your thing, as you have just reminded me, okay, but I will be damned if your head and mine land on the same pillow. Don't even think about something like that."

During the entire time Awu was talking, Nguema Afane was sporting a contemptuous frown; his eyes reflected arrogance. None of this went unnoticed by Awu. Nonetheless, she continued on:

"You and I, we are going to take each day one stitch at a time, with my threads clearly separated from yours even though all of them will belong to the same piece of work. My threads cannot hook up with yours; it might put a wrinkle in our fabric. Let's keep our distance in order to achieve a certain harmony. That's what I'm asking you to do."

"And what about tradition?"

"Tradition is about people, and people won't know because it's a secret."

"And just who do you think I am, Awu? Aren't you going to end up losing respect for me in the end? A man who passes up beautiful things without even trying to touch them is not a man!"

"Me!? A beautiful thing!? Me, your big brother's wife!? And since when am I no longer Mama Awu?"

"Well, since tradition decided so! You are a beautiful thing, Awu!"

"Thing, yes. Beautiful, no! Ah! Death brings such sadness! So Nguema Afane is speaking to me like this today! Oh! Obame Afane! Where are you? Can you hear all this?"

Then, getting up, Awu set the open notebook down on the bed and took herself over to the solid wood table on which a feather pen sat in an inkwell uninterrupted for several months now. With her right hand, she took the pen-holder and made a swollen drop of dark red ink fall into her left hand. Awu put the pen-holder back in the inkwell and, sitting herself across from Nguema Afane, she spread the drop of ink in the palms of both hands and said:

"This is the red ink that your brother Obame Afane used to correct the errors of his children, his students. Look how red my hands are. That dark drop of ink has become bright red like the marks in the margins of this notebook here on the bed. Listen to me. Starting this very instant, the two hands that you see here are going to start correcting a lot of things in my life as sure as my name is Awudabiran'. Normally, you should provide for my needs and those of my children, since we are your things and you are the man; therefore, you are responsible. But that won't be happening. After your brother went on retirement I was the one—yes, me . . . a Thing—who supported your family . . . you, your wives, and children . . . all by sewing extra table linens. I did it out of love for my husband, to raise his spirits, so that life after retirement wouldn't be hell as it very well could have been if I hadn't had that job. I did that to raise his spirits, do you understand? But I see now that his love for you all was one-sided. Not one of you loved him, especially not you. You were jealous of your brother. And you want to take revenge against him after his death. You aren't Obame Afane's brother, you are his enemy. So listen. I swear I will be damned if these hands start working again to help out your wives and children. Consider this as correction number one.

If Nguema Afane was more or less intoxicated at the start of this conversation, Awu's latest words had certainly sobered him up. With frown lines on his face and his mouth agape, he got up and took a step toward Awu, who in turn had to take a step backward just to escape from the odor of palm wine that was violently attacking her nostrils.

"Maybe it's you who are jealous that I have inherited a gold mine from my brother!"

"Ahhhh, now I'm a gold mine!"

"Yes! All your talents are now for me: your fingers, your body, your bed! Everything is mine! Tradition wills it so!"

"Oh, Nguema Afane, the carp sees the fishhook but it will no longer take the bait! And as for correction number two, tradition will not stop my hand the day your head lands on my pillow; look at what color your semen will be. Take a good look, because by the time it spurts out of your body, you will have already left this world to join Obame Afane. This, I promise you!"

With these words Nguema Afane left the bedroom, slamming the door shut. He had avoided answering back without first having had enough time to think about what he would say. It was a crucial moment. He knew that by leaving without saying anything more, he would avoid things that later could not be undone.

For the first time in his adult life, Nguema Afane went weeks without swallowing a single drop of alcohol. He wanted to clear his head. He knew that he was on the verge of a big turning point in his life, and that perhaps it was all up to him.

As for Awu, she no longer sent any more food to Nguema Afane's wives but gladly gave food to his children, who very often showed up at her house during mealtime. Although they were younger than Nguema Afane's oldest two children, Awu's oldest son and her twins had succeeded in teaching each cousin how to be the man of the house, much to the satisfaction of Awu, who was seeking to avoid conflicts between her and her nephews.

Nguema Afane thought and thought hard. Tradition gave him more rights than duties in this whole Obame Afane affair. But he wasn't able to enjoy any of them because of Awu. The entire village knew her as Awu the Obedient. But as far as he was concerned, she was Awu the Fury who, over the course of many nights, had morphed into Awu the She-Devil in his dreams. He pictured himself squeezing her with all his might until he passed out, after which he would slowly regain consciousness again but in another world. Could it be Obame Afane's world?

Nguema Afane kept asking himself all kinds of questions. Should he force Awu to submit to him? If so, could he actually do it? And if he just left her alone, wouldn't he be considered a coward by the village and maybe also by Awu herself? Was he supposed to try to take Awu by force? No . . . she already haunted him; this woman was really almost frightening to him now. And then, hadn't she threatened him with death if he tried to rape her? But what if this was all talk? Surely, no, it couldn't be just talk. Everyone in the village used to say that an angry woman is a very dangerous one; and if she is "light-skinned," she is ten times more dangerous. Moreover, if she has freckles, she really is a she-devil. And this knife that has been said to have disappeared soon after Obame Afane's circumcision, where was it now? Hadn't Obame Afane taken it? If he had, would he have given it to his wife? If so, what would she use it for? Or else, for whom was it meant? No. Awu certainly had to have something in mind that would cost Nguema Afane his life; and those "adherents of tradition" would always be there to lament his loss after he had gone to join Obame Afane.

So he decided to make the best of his bad fortune. Once a week he decided to find out how Awu and her children were doing; he would come during daytime hours, knock first before entering, and sit in the living room. This weekly visit barely lasted an hour. Little did he care what the village thought of him. In any case he had sunk once more into alcoholism, and it had been over a decade now that the villagers had freely made him the butt of their criticism. And when he was drunk (which he never wanted to admit), he used to imagine that Awu might one day see things in a more favorable light.

As for Awu, she remained vigilant. The only reason she complied with the decision of the traditional Council was to remain with her children. But she swore to herself that she would never give her body up to her new owner. As for her spirit, she had sealed it off in an impenetrable place. She counted on keeping it intact for the memory of her husband and for the happiness of her children, girls and boys alike, for whom she hoped that life would be sewn like a chain stitch, with a solid knot at the end. In any case, she was going to watch over them.

Every evening before falling asleep, Awu ensured that the crosspiece of the headboard still locked away her secret. And that reassured her whenever she felt discouraged at having lost her soulmate. This soul was taken away in a ravine at the entrance to the capital. She often saw the image with a clarity that time could never manage to erase—a man and a woman, obviously happy and full of hope, sitting side by side in a packed bus. They were dressed as if they were going to a ball. But the ball they experienced was of a different kind than expected. An aerial ball turned tragic at the end and from which bloomed some strange roses—thick, red, and hot—on the large green leaves of the superb red kaba. And on the delicately starched yellow shirt, red hot ink flowed in abundance, taking away promises and dreams in its wake.

NOTES

1. A *pagne* is traditional African cloth used mostly to make dresses but also table linens and so forth.
2. *Malamba* is Fang for sugar cane wine. *Musungu* is the Punu word for palm wine. Both are traditional beverages locally produced by villagers.
3. The original religion of the Ekang people, which Christian missionaries attempted to eradicate.
4. African drum carved out of wood.
5. Traditional loose-fitting African gown worn by both men and women.
6. Traditional African dress.
7. In the Fang language, this translates as "phantom knife." It refers to a leaf whose edges are as sharp as a knife.
8. Schools in Gabon model the French educational system, so Ada's grade level (*cinquième*) is equivalent to that of a seventh grader, and *collège* would be considered middle school.
9. Assok is a Fang village in the north of Gabon.
10. A traditional African game invented first by the Fang that requires keen mathematical skills to win. It is a board game somewhat similar to chess, whereby each opponent tries to conquer territory indicated by twenty or so holes scattered on a game board. Seeds are placed in the holes to signify that a "territory" has been taken by an opponent.
11. An *atangatier* is a tropical tree native to Central Africa that yields the fruit called *atanga* in Gabon, but the same fruit is called prune in Cameroon. The fruit is blue-purple and shaped like an avocado; this is surely to what Ada is referring in the novel as "blue dates."

PART TWO

1. A Fang interjection showing surprise in a negative and/or serious situation.
2. *Zom ayo* is a plant with extremely bitter leaves that can be consumed as a vegetable or for medicinal purposes.
3. A *nganga* is a spiritual healer of sorts, someone capable of communicating with those from the beyond and who can therefore impart wisdom and knowledge.

4. The *fête du mouton* refers to the slaughtering of sheep in conjunction with the Muslim holiday, *Eid El Kébir* (also known as *Eid al-Adha*), a commemoration of Abraham's sacrifice. The holiday is declared in relation to the Muslim calendar, and therefore its exact date is announced only a very short time in advance.

PART THREE

1. The *corps de garde* is the entry to a Fang village and an important meeting point for visitors and residents alike.
2. Fang interjection.
3. The currency of most countries in West and Central Francophone Africa is the franc CFA, with an estimated value of about 500 CFA to one US dollar.

www.ingramcontent.com/pod-product-compliance
Ingram Content Group UK Ltd.
Pitfield, Milton Keynes, MK11 3LW, UK
UKHW042149060225
454777UK00004B/400